"Maybe I didn't belong here. . . ."

I looked at my hands. I didn't want to look at Endicott as we drove away. But I knew what we were passing anyway. I could see the library out of the corner of my eye, and the playing fields and gymnasium. We drove past McCarter's Woods and I swore to myself, saying every X-rated curse word I knew. Those stupid woods, me sneaking out to meet Marcus, was how this whole mess got started. But then as we rode, I thought that maybe it was for the best. I was tired of this place anyway. Maybe Hagen had done me a favor by giving me this "time to reconsider my approach to conflict." My conflict was with Endicott. Maybe two weeks away was a good thing. Maybe I didn't belong here anyway. . . .

Other Point paperbacks
you will enjoy:

Somewhere in the Darkness
by Walter Dean Myers

David and Jonathan
by Cynthia Voigt

Until Whatever
by Martha Humphreys

Life Without Friends
by Ellen Emerson White

point

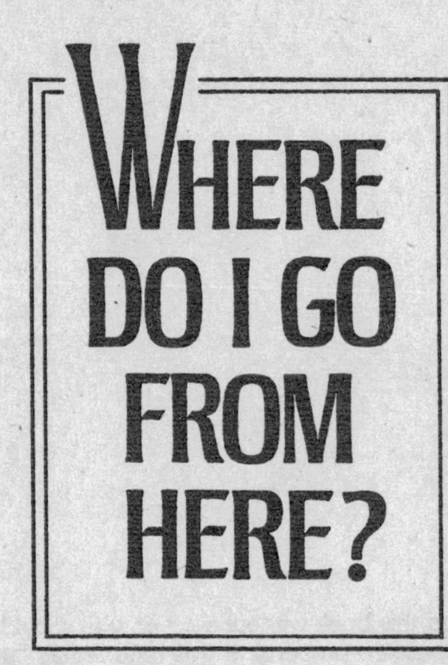

WHERE DO I GO FROM HERE?

VALERIE WILSON WESLEY

SCHOLASTIC INC.
New York Toronto London Auckland Sydney

ISBN 0-590-45607-5

Published by Scholastic Inc. POINT is a registered trademark of Scholastic Inc.

12 11 10 9 8 7 6 5 4 3 2 1   9   5 6 7 8 9/9 0/0

Printed in the U.S.A.   01

For Thembi, Nandi, and Cheo

CHAPTER ONE

"How much money can you get hold of quick?" Marcus Garvey Williams whispered in my ear. He'd been avoiding me ever since school started two weeks before, and here he was asking me for money.

"Have you lost your mind?" I answered his question with one of my own. He *looked* like he'd lost it. His hair wasn't combed, he didn't have on a tie, and there was a wild look in his eyes that I'd never seen before, different from the way he usually looked, so prep-school perfect.

When I'd first come to Endicott Academy last year, I'd known exactly who he was. His picture (since he was one of the four African-American boys in the whole school) had been splattered all over the Endicott brochure . . . the first thing my Aunt Odessa pointed out to me when we first started thinking about me coming here. He'd been leaning against a wall, looking prep, but you could tell he was tough.

Maybe it was the way he held his books or his cocky I-am-bad-do-not-mess-with-me smile. He was definitely a winner, from the top of his head to the tips of his Nikes. Marcus wasn't a TV kind of cute — there was nothing pretty about the boy, but he definitely had the kind of looks that would make you thump your girlfriend on the arm and take another peek before he turned the corner.

I am here to learn as much as I can so that I can make a difference in the lives of my people were the words printed under his photograph. It also said he wanted to be a lawyer and that he was captain of the soccer and chess teams. He was an advanced placement student, which meant he could finish all his major courses by the end of his junior year, and he had a 3.4 average . . . the kind of kid you hate on sight. Except nobody hated him. He was always chill, always in control, which was one of the things everyone admired about him. He was the most popular kid in school, and he'd been my best friend all of last year. Had been, up until this fall.

It was lunchtime. We were sitting at a table in the Endicott Academy cafeteria. As usual, everybody was stopping by to joke with him and still talking about their summer vacations: the parties they went to on the beach; who they saw in Greece; where their families were going during Thanksgiving vacation. Edelston Blaine, torn jeans on her legs, tiny sapphires in her ears, was there, and Devon Wooster, Marcus's best friend. Even Lucinda Spinotta, who calls herself Lucie, grew up in Newark like me (but in the white part), and who makes a point of never speaking or acting like she knows who I am, was sitting at the table acting rich like everybody else. As usual, Marcus was smiling and joking back, except that he was scared, and nobody could tell that but me.

The funny look in his eyes made me feel sorry for him, but I wasn't about to forgive him. I hadn't forgotten last summer. When we left for summer vacation he promised to write. We were even going to get together, check out a movie . . . we made all these big plans. But do you think I ever heard from him? No. Nothing. No letter . . . no call . . . *nada*.

It wouldn't be so bad if *I* hadn't written him. But I had. I wrote the fool *four* times. Four times! By the middle of July I felt like a jerk. By August, I swore if I ever laid eyes on him again, I'd take the first thing I could grab and knock him out. By the beginning of September, just hearing his name made me want to throw up. But here he was, sitting beside me, asking me about money. And here I was, listening to him. I stared at him with my evil eye.

"Nia, listen to me. I'm sorry about the summer. I'll make it up to you, I swear I will. But you're the only one I can count on. The only one I can trust," he whispered to me as soon as everyone had left the table. I didn't say anything for a minute or two, but then my curiosity got the better of me. And that look in his eyes was starting to worry me.

"What's wrong?" I asked finally.

"I can't go into it now, baby. I can't go into it now."

"Baby!" He had never called me "baby" before.

No one except my aunt had ever called me baby before. It was like something on TV. I felt like I should do something to acknowledge it. But I couldn't think of anything to do.

"Can you get hold of some money tonight?" He grabbed my hand and held it. Not like he used to, but like a kid, a kid who was scared of the dark. I didn't like the way it felt. I was starting to get scared, too. Winston, who has been my Aunt Odessa's boyfriend for as long as I can remember, had given me fifty bucks for "emergencies" the last time I'd seen him. You aren't supposed to have emergencies at Endicott Academy, especially ones needing money. Everything — food, uniform, laundry, books — is paid for. But Winston, not wanting to count on the goodwill of folks he didn't know, had slipped me a fifty-dollar bill before I got out of the car he'd rented to drive me here. Now Marcus was holding my hand tight. He wouldn't let it go.

"I've got fifty dollars," I said after a minute.

Marcus looked like he was going to cry. He kissed me gently on my cheek.

"I'll pay you back. I swear I'll pay you back. Can you bring it tonight when everybody's asleep? Maybe around midnight. Under the big tree in McCarter's Woods?"

"McCarter's Woods!?" I said it so loud a couple of kids at the table next to us stopped gossiping and looked up at me in surprise. McCarter's Woods is this clump of trees that separates the girls' and boys' dorms on campus. One of the biggest rules on the books, I mean, the one that's boldfaced *and* italicized, is that you're not supposed to go there. Legend has it that some kids were caught there by Dr. Hagen, the headmaster at Endicott, one Saturday night after curfew and were never seen or heard from again — shipped out before first-period class the next day. Zapped. Disappeared. No one ever knew what they were caught doing. People almost talked about them in whispers. It was spooky. I looked at Marcus like he'd joined the nut squad.

"Why can't I give it to you tomorrow at breakfast?" I asked. That seemed a reasonable alternative.

"I got things to take care of," he said. That faraway look in his eyes again.

Then Charlotte Peters came up, swinging her hips and shaking her head like she belonged in a hair conditioner commercial. Charlotte is one of about six black girls at Endicott (me being one; a Nigerian kid being another). Her daddy is a big-time lawyer who's always being quoted in *Newsweek*, and her mother is a doctor who runs a clinic for women who can't have babies. Her sister had a big write-up in *Jet* magazine when she got married, and Charlotte has the pictures taped on the side of her mirror. Charlotte avoids hanging with me, and even talking to me — except if I'm with Marcus, then I can't shake her.

"Have you seen Lucie Spinotta?" she asked me. "Miss Hildegrande is looking for the two of you. She says she has to see you right away." She smiled at Marcus the whole time she was talking. But he didn't take his eyes off me. He was searching my eyes for an answer.

"See you later on?" he asked, hoping.

"Okay," I said, not so sure.

"Thank you," he said softly, his eyes never leaving mine. Charlotte, shaking her long permed hair, missed the whole thing.

Miss Hildegrande is the admissions lady who handles scholarships. It was funny, up until Charlotte told me that Miss Hildegrande wanted to talk to Lucinda, too, I hadn't known she was on scholarship.

"I saw Lucinda walking off with Ede," I said as I collected my books.

"Would you tell her that Miss Hildegrande is looking for her," Charlotte said to Marcus with a big, phony smile.

"Yeah," Marcus said, snapping back into perfect, helpful prep. He threw me a last look, and Charlotte and I started walking to the office.

Charlotte talked about this cute boy she'd met up at Sag Harbor — this vacation place on the coast of New York — during the summer, and how good Marcus looked, and how she was sick of the Endicott uniform and wanted to break out in these new clothes her daddy had bought her in Rome. I nodded like I was listening, but I was really thinking about that look in Marcus's eyes, what put it there, and why he needed fifty bucks by midnight.

Sometimes I dream about being rich. Not flashy rich like you see on TV: plush condo, red Lamborghini, mink-coat rich. But so rich I could forget about money. So rich I wouldn't have to worry about getting my behind thrown out of here. Rich enough to hand somebody fifty bucks without worrying about ever seeing it again. Edelston Blaine rich. Ever heard of Edelston Foods? Those tiny tins of tuna and salmon that always seem to be on your shelf? Edelston's granddaddy invented them. Edelston ("Ede" to her friends) is so rich she doesn't have to think about it.

Her daddy is an Endicott Academy trustee. Whenever I crack on Edelston, Marcus reminds me that she is probably the reason that I'm here. Those tacky tins of tuna pay for my scholarship — my door to a better life!

Edelston's family has always gone to Endicott. Endicott has been around for about as long as the Edelstons have. Prudence Endicott, the founder, was some wealthy abolitionist, and the Endicott "tradition" of "providing a liberal education to deserving young people in need" is still observed today. Most of the time it's a crock, but sometimes it's for real. It's real for my aunt.

Aunt Odessa, my daddy's sister, is the reason I'm here. She works as a licensed practical nurse. When I'm not here I live with her in our apartment in Newark. She had told my parents to name me "Nia," which is one of the seven Kwanzaa principles and means "purpose" in Swahili. She wheeled and dealed and got me a scholarship here, to one of the "finest prep schools in the nation." I guess she figured I'd have a purpose to my life if I went here long enough. If she were here now, she'd be telling me, "Don't be risking your scholarship for no boy." But she's not here, so I guess I won't worry about her.

And my parents? They've been dead since I was a baby. Aunt Odessa took me in after they were killed in a car accident. I was only about seven months old when it happened, too young to remember them. I guess you could call me an orphan, but I've never thought of myself as being one, never felt like one, either, even though sometimes I talk to my parents before I go to sleep at night. I think about them a lot, too. Like at Christmas or on my birthday and sometimes when I get mad at my aunt. It's like this deep, weird feeling creeps up on me and I miss them more than anything else in my life. But at the same time, I don't know who it is I miss. Being an orphan can have its advantages, though. You can use it for shock value every now and then when somebody's getting on your nerves. When you drop it in a conversation, everybody looks at you like you just did something to get in the *Guinness Book of Records*, especially around here.

But if people at Endicott knew all the facts of my life, about my living with my aunt over a Chinese restaurant in Newark, and not having any other living relatives, they'd probably think I was stranger than they think I am already. Everyone at Endicott Academy, you see, seems *Cosby Show* perfect. Charlotte with her mom, dad, brother, house in Upper Flatburgh, and summer place in Sag Harbor. Edelston Blaine with her millions. Even Edwina, the Nigerian kid, was related to a prime minister before she got thrown out of her country. So I don't say too much about my life before Endicott, not because I'm ashamed but because I don't feel like explaining. It gets too complicated. But sometimes I miss everybody so much it hurts.

I miss Aunt Odessa sitting at the kitchen table, reading the paper and drinking coffee in the morning. I miss the smell of Lin Wan's China Wing restaurant downstairs. I miss our whole apartment, old and small and decrepit as it is. The whole five rooms would fit into a corner of the dining hall here. I miss my girls — my best friends — Debra and Malika — more than I ever thought I would. Sometimes I wish I were home.

That's strange because Debra and Malika used to tell me *they* wished they were here. Especially when I showed them pictures of Endicott, the "Training Ground for Tomorrow's Leaders." It's like someplace off a postcard, this place is. You look out your window and all you see is hills. It's only about thirty-five miles from where I live, but you'd think it was a different planet. The grass is so green in spring you can smell it. In winter when you open the window, a crisp, clean coldness hits your face so pure and strong it has a taste. They've got courtyards filled with tubs of flowers in spring and ice sculptures in winter.

You step into rooms at Endicott, any room, and it's like walking into a museum: wooden beams on the ceilings, leather chairs in the library, and windows so old you can hardly see through them, and that funny, moldy smell that old places have. It's like stepping back in time. My first week here, last year when I was a freshman, before I met Marcus, it really took me out.

For one thing, this place is full of rules. They got rules telling you when to go to class and when to study. Rules saying what you can wear where and how long you can wear it. They even got rules telling you how long you can pee — everybody's got half an hour in the bathroom each morning between seven and seven-thirty. But the biggest rule they got (the one I'm breaking as soon as lights go out tonight) is the rule about "fraternizing" with "unauthorized people in unauthorized places." In other words, meeting Marcus Williams in McCarter's Woods at midnight. They'd throw me out if they knew I broke that one. They'd throw him out, too, even though he's a "super kid" and everybody loves him.

CHAPTER TWO

The day went quickly; it always does when you dread doing something, and I dreaded meeting Marcus in McCarter's Woods. The whole afternoon I was in a daze and couldn't concentrate. I don't remember half of what happened.

I was a wreck when night came and it was time to go. When I closed my door at 11:45 and headed for the hall, my legs were shaking so hard I could hardly walk. My throat was tight. I took a few steps at a time, sneaking around corners, making sure nobody saw me. I'd put my nightgown on over my clothes, figuring that if somebody caught me before I got out of the dorm I could close my eyes and pretend I was sleepwalking. It sounds dumb now, but at the time it seemed like a good idea. That tells you the kind of shape I was in, going to meet Marcus in McCarter's Woods.

Our dorm is like a big house. You've got to walk

down three flights of stairs and through the kitchen, which we use to pop corn and make snacks, to make it out the door. I guess it's supposed to be cozy, to make you feel like you're home, but my first week here last year I just got lost. I'd finally gotten to know which stairs creak, and as I crept downstairs I stepped over the first one — the noisy one. But, naturally, when I got to the second one, I tripped on the hem of my gown and nearly fell all the way down.

"Who's there?" yelled Mrs. Rogers, the lady who is the resident counselor and runs the dorm.

"Is there someone there?" She rushed the words all together like my aunt does when somebody rings the doorbell late at night and she's kind of scared.

"It's Nia."

"Who?" Mrs. Rogers asked real loud, so I figured she didn't have her hearing aid on.

"Nia!"

"Oh, child! You scared me half to death." She breathed a sigh of relief as she stepped into the hall clutching her robe. With the night cream smeared all over her face and her hair all messy, she looked like a punked-out Mrs. Butterworth, that lady in the apron who has the syrup named after her. "What are you doing down here in the kitchen at this time of night?"

"I was fixing a glass of milk. I can't sleep. Sometimes a warm glass of milk puts me right to sleep!" Actually warm milk makes me sick to my stomach, and I never have trouble sleeping. The minute my head hits the pillow I'm a goner. But I delivered this lie with a sweet little grin. I'm not a good liar, so I watched Mrs. Rogers's face to see if she could tell. I always figure whenever I'm lying folks can see straight through me.

Lucky for me, she had left off her glasses with her hearing aid; she couldn't see my face good. For effect, I got out a carton of milk, poured it into a pan, and put it on the stove. When it began to bubble, I poured it into a cup. Mrs. Rogers yawned and turned to go back to her room.

"Okay, dear. Sweet dreams. Make sure you turn off the stove." She closed her door and switched off her light. I waited for a few minutes and then poured the milk down the sink.

I felt bad. I don't like to lie, especially to somebody I like, and I like Mrs. Rogers. I felt like I was taking advantage of her. Standing in the kitchen with the chilly fall air whipping around my ankles, I was starting to get mad at Marcus again. Mad because he hadn't seen fit to tell me *why* I was making this dangerous trip in the middle of the night to McCarter's Woods — risking my well-being *and* my scholarship. Mad because he hadn't seen fit to call me all summer. Mad because it was a quarter of twelve and it was cold and I really wanted to be snuggled up to Dandelion, this stuffed yellow penguin I've had since I was a baby. I wanted to be warm under the comforter my aunt had bought me at Fortunoff's last summer. I sat down at the kitchen table. Let the fool get his money somewhere else, I said to myself. But then, I thought about last fall and I knew I had to keep my promise to him.

* * *

"Some of these dudes have Polo stitched on their drawers," were the first words Marcus Garvey Williams said to me. It was at the beginning-of-the-year square dance, the first social "event" at Endicott Academy. They hold it to welcome new students. I was leaning against a wall in the gym checking it out, trying to look cool. I'd never been to a square dance before, and it was the corniest thing I'd ever seen. I didn't know what the calls meant; I didn't like the music; I hated the way everybody was smiling; and I felt stupid, just standing there watching. I tried to look mean so nobody would ask me to join in. Nobody did. Except for Mrs. Rogers and Mr. Windsor, the assistant headmaster, Marcus was the first person to talk to me that night. The moment I saw him, I recognized him — the kid in the brochure. So what was he on, some kind of goodwill mission? I ignored him and didn't say anything.

"Hey, Newark. I'm talking to you," he said after a minute. My curiosity got the better of my cool.

"How did you know I was from Newark?" I asked. He looked even cuter in person than he did in the book. I'm usually nervous when I talk to cute boys, and I usually try not to smile because my lips always shake. But I ended up smiling back. And my lips didn't act up.

"I have my ways," he said mysteriously, and he gave me what I came to know as his Marcus glance — a half smile, slightly mocking at first, that turns into a wide, good-natured grin. He looked around, then turned to face me. "Well, how do you like the square dance?"

"Square," I said.

"They do it to help people get acquainted. It's impersonal, and if you join in, it forces you to dance with almost everybody here. But you've got to join in or it doesn't work." I guess that was a dig at me, but I pretended I didn't hear it. He chuckled, then reared back as if he'd forgotten something, and grinned slyly. "By the way, my name is Marcus Garvey Williams."

"I know," I said quickly.

"How?" He looked genuinely puzzled.

"I've got my ways." It was my turn to be mysterious. "I'm Nia Jones."

"Purpose in Swahili. One of the seven Kwanzaa principles. Umoja . . . Ujima. I always thought Nia was the prettiest. Your folks must be into Africa. My father was, and so was my grandmother. That's why she named me Marcus Garvey, after — "

"I know after who," I said quickly, not wanting to be outdone on my knowledge of African-American history. "Winston, my aunt's boyfriend, is Jamaican. He's from St. Anne's Parish in Jamaica, the place where Marcus Garvey was born. He told me all about him."

Marcus Garvey was this great leader who came to New York from Jamaica in the 1920s. He made black folks proud to be themselves by teaching them about Africa and what they could accomplish by believing in their past and future. For as long as I've known Winston, which is as long as I've lived with Aunt Odessa, which is almost as long as I've been around, he's talked about Marcus Garvey.

"My grandmother lives right near where they used to have the parades," Marcus said. "When I was a kid, I used to try to imagine what it must have been like, you know . . . the parades and everything. My daddy's daddy was a Garveyite, one of the dudes that followed him. My daddy's dead."

He said it without missing a beat — the way I told people I was an orphan. We had something in common — he wasn't *Cosby Show* perfect, either. As he turned to wave at somebody across the floor, I noticed a Polo emblem on the collar of his knit shirt.

"A gift from my mom," he said before I could ask. I wondered if he read folks' minds along with everything else. "It cost her lunch for a week, but she wanted me to fit in."

"Do you?"

"Do I what?"

"Fit in?"

"Do you?" He turned the question back on me, giving me a look — half joke, half dead serious — that dared me to lie.

"No," I said bluntly. Even if I'd been a decent liar, I couldn't have lied about *that.* From the moment I'd come into the dorm two days before, until this very moment, standing in the middle of this corny dance, I'd felt like a freak. I had never been anyplace in my life where I was the only kid who looked like me. In the few days that I'd been there, there were lots of things at Endicott that made me feel like I didn't belong — like the way some kids took money for granted, or the way they assumed that you grew up on welfare just because you were black. It made me feel weird. Everytime I did something, I felt people were watching me out of the corner of their eyes.

"It's rough at first," said Marcus, tapping his foot to the music. "The only African-Americans most of the dudes here have ever seen are gardeners or waiters at the country club. My first year here, my roommate thought I was the janitor's helper, asked me to please take a look at the sink. I looked at him like he was out of his mind." He laughed, but it had a hollow ring to it. "We're friends now. I went home with him during Christmas vacation last year, met his mama, his sister, and everyone else." He laughed again. "You get used to it."

I wasn't so sure. If somebody thought I was the janitor's helper after what my aunt went through to get me in here, I'd slap somebody in the mouth first, and ask questions later. But I didn't say anything.

"I don't know if I can ever get used to being the only black kid in the school," I said after a minute. "I've never been the *only* black kid anywhere in my life."

"You're not the only black kid here. What do you call me, William, Turner, and Doug?"

"Boys."

"We're African-Americans."

"You know what I mean. It's not the same."

"How about Edwina?"

"She's African."

"That's black."

"She's *British*!" I said, imitating Edwina's accent.

"Don't forget Charlotte."

"She doesn't count." From the moment I met

Charlotte Peters, I felt like cracking on her. She, along with my homegirl who wasn't a homegirl, Lucinda Spinotta, were the only kids who I was introduced to in the dorm who acted like I was an untouchable. I think my being an African-American reminded Charlotte that she was, too, and she didn't like being reminded.

"You're going to have a rough four years," Marcus said and shook his head sympathetically. I was getting ready to tell him I didn't care what he thought when a tall, blond boy whose face was covered with freckles started shouting Marcus's name from across the room. I could tell he was somebody important. As he walked across the gym, people stopped dancing to let him pass . . . like the Red Sea parting in the *Ten Commandments*, this old-timey film I saw one night on late-night TV.

"Hey, man. Glad to see you back," he said as he gave Marcus that half-grab half-hug that boys always give each other. Marcus hugged him back.

"Hey, man," said Marcus. "I want you to meet my . . . my home girl, Nia Jones. Nia this is Devon Wooster, president of the junior class."

"Homegirl? . . . So you come from this turkey's hometown?" Devon extended his hand and I shook it, smiling self-consciously. Several of the girls from my dorm who had snubbed me when I sat down at the lunch table that afternoon were beginning to check me out. Here I was, a freshman, talking to the president of the junior class. I was beginning to feel like a star, but I tried to act casual. I nodded, too nervous to trust my untrustworthy lips.

"How do you like it so far?" he asked.

"Nice," I managed to squeak out. Devon hardly heard me; he was too busy waving for other people to join us, and about six upper classmen did. Devon introduced me as Marcus's friend. I smiled at everyone and tried to look like I belonged.

"So what's your load look like this year, man?" Devon asked.

"I'm stacking it up so I can coast next year," Marcus answered, patting his foot to the beat.

"Wow, check this dude out!" Devon said to no one in particular. "Here's one of those turkeys who can actually graduate as a junior — like you read about in the crap they send you from Hagen's office." Everybody who was standing around started to laugh, including me, even though I wasn't sure what I was laughing at.

"So what are you doing for Thanksgiving?" Devon asked Marcus as soon as people started clearing away.

"We just got back, and you're talking about getting away?" Marcus asked in mock disbelief.

Devon laughed. "Getting away is *all* I think about. You want to go down to the islands?"

Marcus reared back and gave him the same dramatic look he'd given me when he told me his name. "Man, you think my daddy is running AT&T? I hardly have enough money to get back to New York City to say nothing about the islands. What do you think I am, a rich white boy?"

I looked at Marcus in shock. It didn't seem like the kind of thing you'd say to a friend . . . especially if he *was* a rich white boy.

Devon asked in mock seriousness. "Who are you calling rich white boy?"

"Who *looks* like a rich white boy around here? Do I look like a rich white boy?" Marcus asked, glancing at me with an amused look on his face. I was too uncomfortable to respond one way or the other. "Does *she* look like a rich white boy?" he asked, nodding at me. They started to laugh. I stood there feeling embarrassed.

"Man, don't worry about the money," Devon said reassuringly. "It's completely on me. My dad thinks you're the greatest thing since Michael Jordan, he thinks they should name a pair of sneakers after you. My old lady wants to adopt you, you know, adopt-a-nigger. Like those black kids and that rich white guy on that old TV show in reruns." He nodded at Marcus with a joking there-I-got-you-back look.

I stepped back, my mouth open. Fighting words had been uttered. Where I come from, a white kid doesn't say "nigger" to a black kid without expecting to get his behind kicked. But Marcus didn't flinch.

"No thanks, Dev. I see enough of *you* people around here without hooking up with your family." He said it lightly, but his words cut through the air.

I wasn't sure what to make of either one of them. Here they were, supposedly good friends, insulting each other without even acknowledging it. The world of Endicott was even stranger than I thought.

"Well, think about it, man. You'd enjoy it," Devon

said with a wink. "I hear those island ladies are something else." He gave Marcus a playful punch on the arm and walked away.

"Sure thing, man," Marcus called after him, acting like nothing had happened.

As soon as Devon disappeared, I turned to confront Marcus. I wasn't sure what to say or if I *should* say anything, but my curiosity got the better of me.

"Do you always talk to your white friends like that? Do you let kids call you 'nigger' and not say anything back?" I asked the two questions quickly and bluntly.

"I call him worse things than that," Marcus said. "Devon and me joke like that sometimes. It's like thumbing your nose at the race thing — the kind of stuff that hangs most people up. Like they do on *In Living Color*. It's no big thing. If you get mad about stuff like that, you'll be mad around here all the time."

"Well, I'd better pack my bags and go home before this dance is out," I said quietly, and I meant it.

"No, just pick your battles, that's all. There's plenty of other stuff that will get on your nerves."

"Like what?"

Marcus shrugged, and his eyes flickered for a second, and then he turned his attention back to the dance floor.

"Ever been to the islands?" he asked after a few minutes, not answering my question.

"Staten Island."

"I've never even gotten *there*." He looked at his feet, and then took a deep breath like he was thinking about something serious. Suddenly he looked sad, and it surprised me. Standing here, in the middle of the square dance, he was as cool and sophisticated as he'd seemed in the booklet. A moment before, he'd been smiling and joking the same as Devon and the others. With his knit Polo shirt, tailored pants, hand casually in his pocket, and head cocked back like he owned the world, he looked like an Endicott man — in technicolor. I wondered what *he* had to be worried about.

We stood listening to the music for a few minutes, and I started thinking about the dances in my old school back home. I missed Malika teaching me some new dance she'd learned, and Debra sneaking into the girls' room to smoke a cigarette. I missed the music pounding so loud and hard you couldn't sit down, and I missed everybody, even the dumb guys — laughing long, looking good, styling back. I felt like crying. When Marcus spoke, I was thinking hard about myself.

"You forget who you are and treat everyone like you treat the brothers back home and everything is fine. But sometimes stuff happens that gets on your nerves, you know, race stuff . . . money stuff. Sometimes it gets to you. . . . My mother says that no matter what happens, black kids have got to be better. Good won't get it, you've got to be better." He paused for a moment, looking around the gym. "So I'm *always* better." He'd gotten my attention. "I'm glad you're here." He said it softly, looking directly into my eyes for the first time since he'd started talking. "Because nobody else, like Charlotte or the other black kids in my dorm, is really coming from the same place as us, on scholarship . . . no bucks . . . from the hood . . . you know what I mean?"

"Yeah." I knew what he meant.

"Home?" he asked as if we were kids in fourth grade sealing a secret pact.

"Home," I said.

"You want to dance?" he asked. I took his hand and he led me to the dance floor, and before the night was out, I had learned how to square dance and I was having a good time.

So that was the way last year went. Marcus introducing me to his friends, teaching me how to book for exams, showing me the ropes. By the end of the school year, nothing about Endicott scared me. If you'd seen me in my uniform suit and blouse strutting down the hall, talking to kids whose daddies owned cities, you would have thought I lived that way all my life. And when I had doubts about fitting in, or what to say; when I got mad and couldn't handle the pressure anymore or just plain wanted to slap somebody across the mouth because of something ignorant she said, Marcus was there — like they say in that TV commercial about State Farm insurance.

Ever heard of reincarnation? It says that when you die, you don't go to heaven, but come back and live life as someone or something else. In another life, I'm sure that Marcus was my brother. And I owed him.

CHAPTER THREE

So I sat waiting to repay my debt, on a cement bench at the end of a path under a tree in the middle of McCarter's Woods. It was cold and wet. It had started to rain. I was disgusted. I started playing this game, pretending I was a spy waiting for my contact. When I'd left the dorm, I'd taken my coat from under my gown and put it on. Now I pulled the collar up over my ears and slouched down on the bench. I started talking softly to myself like I was talking to another spy. It seems kind of dumb now when I think back, but at the time it kept me company (if you can keep yourself company by talking to yourself). The truth was it was scary out there, and I kept thinking about *Nightmare on Elm Street* and Freddie Krueger — thinking that actually I was dreaming the whole thing and that Freddie was going to reach out from under the park bench, grab me by the ankle, and pull me into the ground.

Then Marcus came up behind me and patted me on the shoulder. I almost died. "Aauggh!" I screamed. The scream was way down in my throat, not a cute-sounding scream like the girls have on TV.

"Nia, is that you?" he laughed. I could have punched him.

"Who else do you think it is sitting out here like a fool in the middle of the night, freezing her butt off?" He sat down beside me. I noticed he had changed his clothes, but he had that same look in his eyes, too.

"Here." I handed him the money. He got serious all of a sudden, then stuffed it into his pocket without looking at it, like it was the last thing in the world he wanted to talk about.

"Thanks."

"I want to know what it's for," I said. I'd decided he owed me an explanation. "I know you couldn't tell me before, 'cause everybody was around, but we're alone now, you can tell me."

He looked at me like he was thinking, and I thought he was going to say something, but he didn't. He just looked straight ahead, at this bush that was growing crooked on the other side of the park.

"Do you owe somebody money?" I asked, knowing full well it wasn't that. Marcus made a big deal out of never borrowing money from people.

He didn't say anything, just stared.

"Are you lending it to somebody?" But I knew that wasn't it, either. Marcus wouldn't make me go to all this trouble to lend somebody money he knew I didn't have.

"I know you're not buying weed or brew or anything like that," I said. A lot of that kind of stuff goes on at Endicott, although the parents and teachers swear they don't know about it. I didn't think Marcus was into it, but you never know. Somebody's always getting busted for being drunk or spacing out on drugs.

"Be serious," he said.

"What, then?"

"I can't go into it."

"Marcus — "

"Can't you just leave it at that, Nia? I can't go into it. I'll tell you when I can. I'll tell you later."

"When's later? Tomorrow afternoon, next Wednesday, when?"

"You sound like a kid."

"I am a kid."

"Just later." He said it with a finality that told me I was getting on his nerves. I decided to drop it. So we just sat there.

The whole park was hazy, little bits of rainbows clinging to the spiderwebs on trees where the leaves were beginning to change. We started to hold hands. I don't know why, just because we were sitting there, I guess. More comfort than romance. It seemed like time was standing still. I almost forgot that we were breaking the most important rule at Endicott and that we shouldn't press our luck, should start heading back, but I didn't want to leave.

From somewhere we heard the whistle of the train

that comes to Endicott Township from the north — Newark, New York, and points south, upper this and upper that — places I'd never heard about until I got to Endicott. It made me think of home again, of Debra, Malika, and Aunt Odessa.

"Did I ever tell you about the day my daddy left?" Marcus asked suddenly. It took me by surprise.

"No. How long ago did he leave?" I figured he wanted to talk about it. You don't bring up stuff like that unless it's bugging you.

"About five years ago. I was twelve. It was a night like this, rainy, in September. I can remember because I kept worrying about him getting cold and being wet."

"Did you see him leave?"

"Yeah. He thought I was asleep. But I wasn't. I was supposed to be and I didn't want him to yell at me, so I kept my eyes closed. He came in, sat on the edge of my bed for about half an hour, then kissed me on the forehead. I opened my eyes and looked at him and he was crying. It was the first time I ever saw him cry and it scared me."

"I saw my Aunt Odessa cry once," I said. Marcus didn't say anything. Then he started talking again.

"I put my arms around him and I started crying, too. It was like he didn't have to tell me he was leaving 'cause I knew it. Things weren't working out between him and Mom and I'd known he would be going sooner or later."

I was afraid Marcus might start to cry now because he looked so down.

"So then he took this from around his neck and

put it around mine." Marcus showed me these dog tags attached to a peace symbol that he sometimes wore. I had never paid too much attention to them, but I looked at them now.

"He got them during Vietnam. He said that his whole unit was wiped out in a fire fight but the tags kept him safe. He said they'd keep me safe in any wars I found myself in. Safe until he saw me again. Then he went to California. He came back a couple of times, and he and my mom tried to make it together but they didn't. He went back to California and then he died." Marcus looked at the tags, examining them closely as if he were seeing them for the first time. Then he reached into his pocket and took out a book.

"I thought you might want to check this out," he said, handing me this old dog-eared copy of *The Autobiography of Malcolm X*. "Williams is going to give you a choice of reading this and something by this dude named Tom Wolfe in Literature from the 1960s next semester. Read this one. Begin it now and get a head start on it."

"That book looks like it's been through a war," I said.

Marcus chuckled, "It has, it belonged to my dad, he took it to Nam with him. Take care of it, it's got a history."

"It looks like it," I said. "You sure you don't want to keep it? I can get a copy next semester."

"No, take it," he said as he thrust it into my hand. "A gift. From me to you!" He said it with a Marcus flourish and a little bow. Marcus was always messing around. He was even kidding around when we walked back to the dorm, making his voice sound like Freddie Krueger's, and teasing me about being scared. I stuffed the book into my pocket and we laughed and carried on until we got within hearing distance of the dorm. Then he kissed me quickly on the lips, more a brotherly peck than the kind of kiss you dream about (but it was the second that day), and I thought about that kiss when I snuggled back under my comforter. I wondered what was bugging Marcus. But then, typical me, I forgot about him and started thinking about what they were going to have the next morning for breakfast in the cafeteria. I thought about cinnamon sweet rolls and how good they taste. Then I rolled over and went to sleep.

The day started out normal enough. I was daydreaming as I brushed my teeth over the sink in the bathroom, hoping that Winston had sent me another one of his money gifts. I was so lost in my own thoughts, looking at myself in the mirror, I wasn't listening to what Lucinda Spinotta and Edelston Blaine were talking about when they came into the bathroom.

"Hey, Nia, what's going on?" Ede asked. "Can I get your Am Lit notes later on?"

"Sure," I said. "No problem." Ede's always kind of friendly to me and, except for the fact that she's rich, she's really pretty cool.

Lucinda squeezed out "Good morning." Lucinda gets on my nerves. She's always trying to get in tight with Edelston and her girls, always up in their faces, visiting their rooms, playing up to them. I guess with a name like Lucinda, she's bound to have a problem. I started brushing my teeth, but real easy. Being naturally nosy, I listened to what they were saying.

"I'll bet it was drugs," said Lucinda. "It's always drugs with them." I didn't like the way she said "with them" or the cozy us-against-the-ignorant-masses look she gave Ede. For Lucinda, "them" always means us black folks. But I decided to let it slide. After all, nobody was talking to me. I started to gargle with my Listermint, spitting it out with a noisy vengeance.

"I don't know. Marcus wasn't that type. He never . . ."

I didn't hear anything else because my heart was up in my throat; I started choking on the Listermint and Ede came over and hit me on the back a couple of times.

"You okay?" she asked quickly. Lucinda just watched me choke.

"Ede, what did you say about Marcus?"

"You didn't hear yet? He's gone."

"What do you mean he's gone?"

"He left last night after curfew. He's gone, nobody knows where he is."

It was like somebody had punched me in the stomach. I felt my heart pounding for a minute, then it got tight, like I was going to throw up. I felt scared, real scared.

"Nothing happened to him because all his clothes are gone. He planned it," Lucinda said, turning back to the mirror, combing her hair like nothing had happened, like she was talking about something that just went down in class.

I didn't want to talk to them. I couldn't. How could he be gone? I went back to my room and sat on my bed. I'm not even sure how I got back there. I watched the clock tick, and held Dandelion as tight as I could. I knew I had to get ready to go to class, but I couldn't move.

Maybe something had happened to him. Maybe I was the last person to see him alive. I thought about how bad he'd looked. He really hadn't been himself since we'd been back. I started thinking about how he'd given me his book, and how they say when a kid is going to kill himself, he gives his most precious things away. Then I thought about Johnston Pryor.

Johnston Pryor was this kid who killed himself last year in the dorm. The pressure had finally gotten to him and one night, around three o'clock in the morning, he jumped off the roof of the boys' dorm. They canceled classes the next day and everybody had to stay in their rooms while they cleaned everything up. But some kids saw the body and told everybody else what it looked like sprawled out on the pavement. They called in this psychologist to talk about it and they gave Johnston a memorial. Everybody still felt like the school had killed him, so a couple of kids tore up the cafeteria. Everybody whispered and talked about it for weeks afterwards, saying it was drugs. Drugs and the pressure. That he couldn't take it. He was in my sixth-period music class. He was kind of weird-looking, kind of a nerd with glasses and a crewcut that was so blond it almost looked white, but I liked him because he liked Public Enemy. He was one of the few kids here who even listened to them before they got real popular.

I didn't think that Marcus would do something like that . . . kill himself. Marcus was too cool to jump out of a window around here and have kids standing around gawking at him sprawled out on the sidewalk like a squashed tomato. I *knew* Marcus wasn't dead. There wasn't any body, and his clothes were gone, too.

Somebody knocked on my door and I went to answer. It was Charlotte Peters.

"Did you hear? Did you hear? It's soooo embarrassing," Charlotte said.

"What are you talking about?" I asked in a haze.

"It's too embarrassing. There's only a few us here and when somebody does something like this it makes us all look bad."

I looked at her in amazement. She saw the surprise in my face and figured I hadn't heard.

"You know what happened, don't you? You heard that Marcus Williams — "

"I heard," I said, turning away angrily. "So what!"

I didn't mean so what that he was gone, because I was so worried I couldn't even think straight. I was disgusted with her for being concerned about Marcus because it might affect the way people thought about *her.* It made me sick to my stomach.

"So what?" she screeched dramatically. "He's gone! The great Marcus Garvey Williams has split! He's thrown away everything. Everything! My parents would kill me. They'd kill me!" she kept mumbling to herself as she walked down the hall toward the Nigerian kid's door, shaking her head. I closed my door and sat down on my bed again. And then I started to cry. Charlotte was right; he'd thrown everything away. And one thing was for sure. I'd made it possible. I'd met him in McCarter's Woods at midnight. It was my fault. I'd given him the money.

CHAPTER FOUR

For the rest of September and on into October, you couldn't get from one spot in Endicott to the other without hearing Marcus's name, and how he had snuck out like he had. It was like he had done something low-down and dirty, like leaving Endicott was one of the worst things you could do, like shooting the president or something. Everybody had something to say about it, even kids who usually wouldn't give you the time of day would sidle up to you after class and put in their two cents' worth.

His best friend Devon asked me if I knew anything about it, and I could tell he was as worried as me. He kept saying he couldn't understand how Marcus could leave and not even say good-bye. He was really hurt. When we talked about it, he almost started crying, and I got mad at Marcus all over again. But at least he had said good-bye to *me*. I had that to hold onto and remember. I'd never thought about it, but I guess he'd felt closer to me than to anybody else. I know I felt that way about him.

Everyone seemed to be talking about drugs — everything from how Marcus was a big-time pusher to how he was strung out and going to meet a connection. It was like they were talking about a different person, somebody they hadn't known for three years. Like they'd taken who he was and pushed and pulled him around like he was Play-Doh, to fit into some mold they'd made for him. I couldn't believe what was happening. It was like me and Dev were the only ones who wanted to remember Marcus like he really was.

Lucinda, my girl from Newark, had more to say about it than anybody else. Every time I'd see her head of short, curly hair bobbing ahead of me in the hall or in the cafeteria, I'd pull back so I couldn't hear what she had to say. I almost hated her. But then I was starting to hate everybody. Charlotte had become a royal pain. She was always talking about how embarrassing it was because Marcus was a black kid. White kids didn't feel like it shamed everybody white when something bad happened to a white kid. Endicott, the whole place, was starting to get on my nerves.

I imagined that what they were saying about Marcus they really thought about me, too. I would come into my room after class and just sit and think about home. I wondered what people would say if *I* disappeared like Marcus had. Once I actually packed my bags and was thinking about going, and then I realized I didn't have any money to go anywhere anyway, so I just unpacked and went to bed. But just putting my clothes in my suitcase made me feel better.

I felt like I didn't fit in anymore. People still said hello and stuff like that, but it wasn't the same. Maybe it was my imagination but nobody seemed to be talking to me like they used to and when they did, I couldn't think of anything to say back. I sat by myself in the cafeteria. I was sick of people talking about Marcus and his disappearance. He had become Marcus the bad. It scared me how easy his image changed. I was scared mine was changing, too.

I couldn't stop trying to figure out why he'd left. I'd sit on my bed, open my books, and stare into space. Somebody would knock on my door and I wouldn't answer. I guess Mrs. Rogers told some of the kids on my floor to look out for me, because a couple of girls came by my room to talk to me, to make sure I was okay. I didn't want to see them so when I heard their voices I turned off my light and crawled under the covers. I'd decided I was born alone and there was no reason I couldn't stay alone. It was time for me to start hanging tough. And that's when the mess started with Lucinda.

We were reading *Huckleberry Finn* in English class. Mr. Snowdon, my English teacher, is this tall, thin guy with gray hair. He always likes to joke around, and I liked him until we started reading this book, but now I wasn't so sure. He had given this long, drawn-out speech before we started to read it, telling us how *The Adventures of Huckleberry Finn* was the great American novel and all, and the language they used was "dated" and it was published only about twenty years after slavery, and that they used the word *nigger* in conversation, not to insult anybody. He explained that "Jim" was like the hero of the book and everything, but all those "niggers" in the book started making me sick. Nigger this . . . nigger that . . . nigger, nigger, nigger . . . grating on my nerves. Me and Charlotte and Doug, this black kid who was in Marcus's class, just looked at each other and rolled our eyes; it was getting to them, too. It got to the point where I didn't even hear any other words that Mark Twain had written. All I heard was "nigger." I hated that book.

I guess something just snapped, after sitting there for forty-five minutes listening to the "niggers" roll off Snowdon's tongue. Marcus would have helped me deal with it; he had a way of joking about people being prejudiced that would cool me out, but Marcus wasn't there. Anyway, me and Charlotte were standing around talking about it after class. And that's when things got funky.

"I'm going to call my parents tonight," Charlotte said. "There's no reason for us to have to put up with that language. It's not fair for our parents to pay all this money . . . some of us anyway," she said, with a condescending jab at my being on scholarship. "It's just unfair."

Despite her comment about my being on scholarship, she was right. Maybe Charlotte was finally getting real. I came out of my depression long enough to give her a high-five sign. She was as mad about this "nigger Jim" stuff as me. I slapped her on the back — homegirl style. Then I got this bright idea; the first time my mind was working since Marcus had left.

"I think we should write a letter to Snowden telling him how we feel, send a copy to Dr. Hagen, and then boycott class until they give us something else to read," I said. "That's what we should do." I got excited just thinking about it.

"If we explain how painful it is, how disgusting to sit there in a room full of kids from different ethnic backgrounds and listen to that stuff maybe they won't read it anymore, maybe we can read something else, anything that won't be embarrassing," Charlotte added. There were one or two new black kids who had come in the freshmen class. They stopped by on the way to their new classes and listened to what we were saying. A couple of white kids stopped by to see what was going on.

"It's like when they read *The Merchant of Venice* last year, you know how you felt when they were talking about Jews," Charlotte explained to Sarah, one of her good friends. Sarah nodded her head in agreement. But then Lucinda and Ede strolled by.

"Those minorities . . ." I heard Lucinda say as she passed. My ears pricked up. "They're always up to something," she said, finishing her sentence.

"Lucie, don't say stuff like that," Ede said in a hushed voice. "They'll hear it . . ." Too late. I'd heard it.

"What?" I said so loud everyone turned around and looked at me.

"I wasn't talking to you," Lucinda said. But then, as if she had a second thought, she added, "But I'm going to tell you what I think anyway. I just overheard what you two were talking about and I have to tell you, if you do something like that, I'm going to protest, too."

"Nobody's talking to you," I said. "I'm talking to Charlotte, so mind your own business." I waved her out of my way and turned back to Charlotte, whose face had gone red.

"Well, anyway, Charlotte, like I was saying before . . ."

"This is *my* business because this is *my* school," Lucinda said. "You people always have to get your way," she said.

" 'You people'!? What are you talking about?" I asked. "I don't like the damn book, it's embarrassing to African-Americans, and I don't want to read it."

"You don't have the right to dictate what the majority wants. You're just a minority."

"I'm not a minority, I'm an African-American," I said, getting mad. That majority-minority business gets on my nerves. Marcus used to say that when you started calling people "minorities" instead of what they were, it gave them a bad mind set, made them feel they were "small people." Minorities is all in the way you look at it. It's all subjective; everybody is a minority somewhere.

"*You're* a minority in Newark, Lucinda," I added without missing a beat. Lucinda turned bright red. I guess she'd never told Ede that she was from Newark like me.

"Newark is not important," she hissed back at me in a hoarse whisper. "What's important is the way you people try to stamp on everybody else's rights!"

"What do you mean 'stamp' on other people's rights? I have rights, too. I have the right not to have to read some book if I think it insults me and other black people."

"The problem is everything you read that's any good will probably insult black people," she said with a little toss of her head. "You people are so insultable." That brought a snicker from somebody in the crowd.

I was so mad I felt like crying, but I wasn't about to do that. Charlotte looked like she was getting ready to cry, too. I knew I couldn't depend on her to help me. Ede had an embarrassed look on her face and she was trying to pull Lucinda away, but she wasn't budging.

"That just goes to show how ignorant you are," I said. "You don't know anything about the history of African-Americans or the kind of garbage we've had to take from people like you."

It was getting ugly. I could feel the tension but I couldn't stop. "You're just like me, Lucinda. You're nothing but a poor kid from Newark, trying to pretend she's something she ain't. You're worse than the dumbest crackhead on the scariest corner in the worst block in the Central Ward. There's no excuse for *you* not making it. You're white. What's your problem?"

Lucinda turned even redder than she had before.

There was silence, absolute silence. *She* was almost crying now.

"Give you people a chance and you always blow it," she said. I turned around to leave, dramatically shaking my head in disgust. If that was all she could come up with it was pathetic. But then she added the clincher: "Just look at the great Marcus Garvey Williams. It's like my dad says, 'You can take the kid out of the ghetto but you can't take the ghetto out of the kid.' " A gasp went up from the crowd.

She had hit me in the one spot that was tender. She had attacked Marcus and through him me and every other kid who had tried to make something of himself or herself. I felt numb for a minute, and then I went crazy.

I grabbed her hair as hard as I could. She screamed and slapped me in the face, and started pulling my hair. I slapped her back, and she tossed me on the ground, tearing my uniform. I ripped a button from her blouse, then I sat up and punched her in the stomach. She punched me in the nose, and I hit her in the mouth.

I haven't been in a fight, a real hair-pulling, face-scratching, spitting fight since I was in fourth grade, and this was definitely one of those. I'd been known as a pretty good fighter back in the day, but Lucinda definitely held her own. I got in one last hit before Mr. Snowdon came running out of the room, screaming and waving his hands, and pulled us apart.

A crowd had gathered by then. I was too mad to even care or be embarrassed. We were both crying, and my nose was bleeding. Snowdon grabbed each of our arms like teachers do when you're in kindergarten.

"*Ladies,*" he said, emphasizing the word as if he were hoping that we would begin to act like ladies. "Ladies! That is enough. Enough! I want you both to report to Mrs. Rogers until further notice." Everybody was staring at us as we walked away.

Lucinda and I walked to the dorm like two fighters just out of the ring — silently, with our fists clenched. I could hear everybody whispering, but when I looked around, the crowd was just a blur. When we got back to the dorm, Mrs. Rogers gasped when she saw us.

"Nia! Lucinda! What happened?" She kept saying it over and over again like it was a chant, and shaking her head. Neither of us said anything. I couldn't look her in the face. Mr. Snowdon had walked behind us the whole way. I was so out of it, I hadn't even realized he was there. I guess he was scared we'd start fighting again. He pulled Mrs. Rogers aside and they started talking in low voices.

"I think you girls both better go to your rooms," Mrs. Rogers said firmly when they were finished talking. I went, avoiding everybody's eyes as I climbed the stairs. When I got to my room, I slammed my door closed and locked it behind me. I didn't know it then, but the worst was yet to come.

CHAPTER FIVE

It was four o'clock, four hours after the "incident" and two hours before dinner, when we were summoned to the headmaster's office. I had never been in Dr. Hagen's office before and I never want to go there again as long as I live. The closest I'd gotten to it was his assistant's office when I was accepted into Endicott.

Dr. Hagen's office is big and old and plush. It has the smell of death. The man looks like a mummy. His head is bald, and he's got these tiny little teeth. He's only a few inches taller than me, but when you see him sitting behind that big desk, he looks as big as a basketball player. Lucinda and I walked in together, the fight gone out of both of us. Nobody said anything for a minute. Then Hagen spoke.

"To say I am disappointed with the both of you would be a mild statement to make." His voice was deeper than I thought it would be. He was so small

I thought it would sound wimpy, but it boomed.

"You both are very special girls. You're bright, you're ambitious, you're determined to make it. But when I hear of something like this, this fighting in the halls, this name-calling, these ethnic insults that demean all of us, I'm at a loss for words."

So was I. I couldn't look up. I wanted to sink into the floor. Hagen didn't seem to notice. He was on a roll.

"You might like to know that I have called your parents. Lucinda, I have spoken with your mother. Nia, I have spoken to your aunt. I have explained the situation to them and what I believe to be the best way to handle it."

Oh, God. I thought to myself. Aunt Odessa knows. This may sound weird, but despite Dr. Hagen's words, and the fact that I couldn't look the man in the eye or lift my head, I hadn't really felt bad until I heard him say Aunt Odessa's name.

"I have decided to suspend you both for two weeks, the rest of this week and the following. If within those two weeks you feel that you will be able to abide by the rules we have here at Endicott, you can, if you choose, return to Endicott Academy on Monday, November 4." The "if you choose" stayed in the air like a bad smell. I gasped. Lucinda started to cry.

"I advise you to use your two weeks away from this institution as a period of meditation — a time to reconsider your approach to conflict. I need not tell you that fighting is never, never tolerated at Endicott Academy. If you return, we will see how you conduct yourselves. You will both be on probation.

"I will leave it up to you and your instructors to plan a suitable way for you to make up the work you miss." He paused, both for effect and to pour a glass of water from a silver pitcher on his desk. Lucinda and I studied the water as it flowed into his glass. He took a slow, leisurely drink, then cleared his throat and started in again.

"If this should ever happen again your expulsion will be permanent. Your families will be here to pick you up this evening. I will see you both here in my office on November fourth at nine o'clock sharp, if you decide to return." He stood up and dismissed us with a grand, royal wave of his hand.

I don't remember how I got back to my room. I just remember I sat there, staring at the floor for a while. I didn't feel like crying. I didn't feel like doing anything. Somebody knocked, I guess it was Mrs. Rogers, but I didn't say anything.

"Nia," she said softly. "Are you all right?"

"Yeah," I said after a minute. I didn't want her coming in; I didn't want to see anybody.

"Your aunt's on the phone," she said softly. That was the last thing in the world I wanted to hear.

"Would you tell her I can't come to the phone?" I said. I had never in my life asked anyone over sixteen to lie for me.

Mrs. Rogers didn't say anything for a long time.

"Nia," she said gently. "You're going to have to face her sooner or later."

"Make it later," I said. "I don't want to come out now."

"Okay," she said.

A few minutes later she came back and told me that Aunt Odessa would be there to pick me up at six. I wondered if that was Mrs. Rogers's doing. Everybody would be in the cafeteria eating dinner then and I wouldn't have to face anybody. My aunt got off at six so she was probably leaving work early. I started to feel worse. Here she was leaving work so she could pick me up because I had gotten my butt expelled.

I didn't want to start crying, so I didn't. I'm real disciplined like that sometimes. I just decide I'll hang tough and I can keep from crying. But it was getting hard. I started looking for my stuff and putting it into my bag. I picked up Marcus's *Autobiography of Malcolm X*, and almost got mad at him again, then I threw it into my bag. I wasn't going to think about what went down. I figured if I just forgot about it, it would almost be like it hadn't happened. I packed carefully, folding things just so and putting them into my suitcase. When everything was in, I put Dandelion on top. I didn't close my bag right away. This is dumb, but I don't like to close him up. But I sure didn't want to leave the dorm building holding him in my arms, so I just left the bag open, so he could breathe.

I didn't want to go out of my room, so I figured I'd just leave my soap and toothbrush and stuff in the bathroom.

I could hear everybody coming back from class, talking and laughing. A couple of people stopped for a minute at my door, but nobody knocked and I held my breath. I didn't want anybody to know I was in the room. Then I started crying. I cried about everything. About Marcus, and the fight, and the things I knew kids would say about me when I left, and about disappointing my aunt 'cause I'd gotten thrown out for two weeks. In all the time I'd been here, I'd never heard of anyone being put out of school — even for a day. I cried so loud and long I didn't hear my aunt when she knocked at the door. So she started knocking real loud, like she thought I had killed myself or something. I got up quick and let her in.

Aunt Odessa looked at me without saying anything. Then she just shook her head. I had halfway expected her to smack me across the face, or yell at me, or curse me out (even though I've never heard my aunt curse but once).

"I don't have to tell you how this makes me feel. How ashamed I am of you," she said.

"No," I said. "You don't have to tell me." I didn't want to look at her face. I could feel her eyes burning into me.

She sighed, real deep and sad and low and grabbed one of my bags. "Do you have everything you want to take?" she asked.

"Yeah."

"Come on then, Winston's downstairs waiting for us."

"How you doin' kid," Winston asked softly as he got out of the car to get my bag. He gave me a playful thump on my arm like he always does. For one horrible minute I thought he was going to ask me about the fifty dollars he gave me, but he didn't say anything. Nobody said anything.

I looked at my hands. I didn't want to look at Endicott as we drove away. But I knew what we were passing anyway. I could see the library out of the corner of my eye, and the playing fields and gymnasium. We drove past McCarter's Woods and I swore to myself, saying every X-rated curse word I knew. Those stupid woods, me sneaking out to meet Marcus, was how this whole mess got started. But then as we rode, I thought that maybe it was for the best. I was tired of this place anyway. Maybe Hagen had done me a favor by giving me this "time to reconsider my approach to conflict." My conflict was with Endicott. Maybe two weeks away was a good thing. Maybe I didn't belong here anyway. Maybe this was my way out.

I settled back in the car that Winston had rented. Suddenly, I felt free. Free as a bird. But I didn't say anything to my aunt. I just kept that feeling to myself.

CHAPTER SIX

When I woke up the next morning, I thought I was back at Endicott. I wondered what they were fixing for breakfast in the cafeteria, and if I had clean underwear to put on, and then suddenly I realized that something was wrong. It smelled like home: leftover Lysol from when my aunt cleans on Saturday morning, Jergens lotion lingering in the bathroom, Chinese food — egg rolls, peppers, onions — from Lin Wan's restaurant downstairs. You could put me anywhere in the world, in the middle of a thousand smells, and I'd be able to tell with one sniff where I was. I opened my eyes and looked around.

Everything was the same. My room was still that funny, peppermint-pink me and my aunt picked out two years ago, and there was still a water stain on my ceiling that looked like a rabbit. When I was little I used to lay in bed scared that it would come alive, hop down, and get me. Lin Wan was starting to cook in his restaurant; I could hear him yelling at his kids in Chinese. I knew Aunt Odessa was in the kitchen, drinking coffee and trying not to smoke a cigarette. I wondered what kind of schedule she was on today. My aunt hadn't talked much on the way home last night. We hadn't even looked at each other.

It was weird being home in the middle of the week. I didn't like the way it felt — like I had done something wrong, which I guess I had. Last summer, my aunt had enrolled me in these special college prep classes at Essex County College, so I'd gotten up early and come home with her. Except for during Christmas and Thanksgiving I hadn't been home during the day since I was little.

I got up and started getting dressed. I was just about to put on my uniform out of habit. Dumb. I balled it up and threw it in the closet. I put on my tightest jeans, screwed my biggest hoop earrings into my ears, and smeared lipstick across my lips. I looked at myself in the mirror and grinned in approval. It was bad enough feeling guilty about being suspended for two weeks — I didn't want to look like Endicott Academy.

I breathed a sigh of relief when I went into the kitchen. My aunt was gone. There was a note saying that she was working a double shift this week and all weekend, and she would be home late. It also said that she was very disappointed in me and not to say anything to her for a couple of days because she was too mad to talk to me. She'd also underlined in red ink that she didn't want me to leave the house.

I guess that was her way of punishing me. Keep me a prisoner and not talk to me. That was okay by me. I didn't want to see anyone or talk to anyone, not even my friends, and I certainly didn't want to talk to my aunt, either. She could have as long as she wanted. I needed a couple of days to cool off, too. Maybe things were finally going my way.

I fixed myself some breakfast, and even made a cup of coffee. I never drink coffee; I don't even like coffee. But I was in an outlaw mood. Then I turned on the TV and watched it non-stop all day. I watched cartoons in the morning and the soaps in the afternoon. The minute I heard my aunt's key in the door at midnight every night, I'd run to my bedroom and pretend to be asleep. I didn't want to face her. I was too embarrassed.

After a couple of days of doing the same thing, I started to feel better. Endicott seemed a thousand miles away and a thousand years in the past. I didn't miss the dorm, the curfew, and not being able to eat when I felt like it. I liked sleeping late and not doing any homework. I liked not having to show I was smart by answering questions to impress teachers, and not having to prove myself to dumb kids who thought I didn't belong there. I liked being completely me. And when I thought about that last talk with Hagen — which I thought about almost every morning before I could get up out of bed, I thought that maybe my answer to his "if you choose to return" just might be "No, I don't choose to return. I choose to be here, happy and lazy in my aunt's apartment above a Chinese restaurant. I choose to let you take your Endicott education and all your money and shove it."

A whole week passed — a week of my aunt working her double shifts and seven days of *Sesame Street* and *Hard Copy* and *Geraldo* and *All My Children* — before my aunt broke her silence. She was off that Tuesday morning, and I could hear her frying bacon and the sound of voices talking low while I brushed my teeth. There was the familiar lilt of a Jamaican accent so I knew that Winston must have stopped by for breakfast. I got dressed quick and went into the kitchen. I figured Aunt Odessa probably wouldn't yell at me as long as he was there. Winston was sitting at the table drinking coffee.

"Good morning," Winston said with a nod. I nodded back. My aunt looked at me, but didn't say anything.

"Well," Winston said after a moment, sensing the calm before the storm. "Thank you for the coffee, Odessa, I'd better be on my way." He walked over to my aunt and gave her a quick kiss on the cheek. He nodded to me. " 'Bye, Little Miss," he said, using the name he hadn't called me in years. I could tell by the way he said "Little Miss" and nodded his head that he knew something was up. My aunt and he had probably been talking about me before I came in.

When he left, me and Aunt Odessa stood facing each other in the kitchen. I went to the stove and heaped up my plate with some biscuits, a fried egg, and bacon.

"Are you ready to talk?" she asked.

"Yeah," I said.

"I want to hear your side of what happened and how you feel about it," she said. She said it nice, like she really wanted to know. It took me by surprise after the way she'd been all week. Maybe she was as sick of the silent treatment as I was, or maybe now she just had time to hear what was on my mind. I sat down and told her the whole thing, about Marcus leaving, the things everybody said, and about the fight. I left out the part about meeting Marcus in McCarter's Woods and giving him Winston's money.

She didn't say anything for a few minutes, then she got up and started putting stuff back in the refrigerator.

"So no one's heard from Marcus at all?"

"No."

"Are you sure it wasn't drugs or something? All kinds of kids are getting mixed up in that mess today and you never know — "

"No, Aunt Odessa!" I said more loudly than I meant to. "No! I know it wasn't drugs. The only reason people even bring drugs up is because Marcus is black. If it had been Devon Wooster or Ede Blaine or somebody like that, no one would even be thinking drugs, but because Marcus — "

"Don't you use that tone of voice with me, young lady," she said, peering at me with squinted eyes over her coffee cup. The peace was broken, I could see it. "No wonder you got thrown out of that school, yelling at people like that. Now you know *I* wouldn't think that boy is a dope fiend because he's black, but I know what drugs can do to a person, I know . . ."

"It wasn't drugs or anything like that," I said, making a real effort to sound polite and calm. "I just got upset because he disappeared and people started getting on my nerves."

My aunt shook her head. "Well, honey, *people* may have been getting on your nerves, but *you're* the one who's sitting around here out of school."

I hate it more than anything when Aunt Odessa gets that I-told-you-so tone in her voice. I was afraid of saying something fresh so I looked down at my plate.

She started nodding and mumbling, talking more to herself than to me. "When are you going to learn? When are you going to learn? You can't lose it every time somebody says something dumb. There are other ways to fight besides with your fists! You were there to get an education. And *now* look at you!"

"But — "

Aunt Odessa rose halfway out of her seat and glared at me. If looks could kill, I would have been laying across the kitchen table. And at that minute, I realized there was still more to come.

"There are no buts . . ." she said. "What if Sojourner Truth had reacted to every dumb comment somebody made about her? Or Frederick Douglass? What if they had been set off their course by nonsense? Where would we be? What about Dr. King, walking through Cicero? Now I know that you didn't have to face anything like Dr. King faced, did you? Did you? Answer me, girl!"

"No," I said quietly.

"Even me. If I jumped off the handle every time somebody at work said something dumb you wouldn't be sitting there getting ready to stuff your face with bacon. Words can't kill you. They can hurt you but they can't kill you! You've got to keep your eyes on that prize. Everybody's got a prize. Yours, young lady, is to keep your scholarship and make it through Endicott Academy so you can get a scholarship to college. That's what your prize is, Nia. Because I can't pay for college. I just don't have enough money."

I felt like crying. I took a bite of biscuit but it tasted like cardboard. I wasn't hungry anymore.

"Aunt Odessa," I said finally. "I just didn't fit in anymore. I hated it. You just don't understand what it was like — not having what other kids have. Aunt Odessa, you remember how it was at Parents' Visiting Day?" I could tell by her eyes that she hadn't forgotten.

Charlotte's mother had come to the annual event in her furs. Ede's mother had been in her Adolfo suit and they'd looked my aunt over, determined who she was and where she was from, and dismissed her with pleasant, cool smiles. Even the suit my aunt had paid all that money for at Macy's hadn't fooled them. They knew she wasn't "important" in the scheme of things — at Endicott or in the world — just some scholarship student's aunt. They'd made conversation, but they didn't talk to her like they talked to each other. She and Winston hadn't even stayed for the whole thing. It had been typical, typical of Endicott, and I'd hated the school for it.

Aunt Odessa turned away, not looking me in the eyes. "Nia, not having money and those kinds of things shouldn't matter, they — "

"They shouldn't matter, but they do. You really don't understand, do you?" I asked. "You don't understand what it's like being the only poor kid in a rich school — the only black kid in a white world."

"I just know that you've made me ashamed of you." She had the last words — as usual.

I thought about trying to make her see my side of things again. But I didn't feel like arguing, so I didn't say anything. I threw my food in the trash, went into the living room, and turned on the TV. I sat there watching TV — watching until afternoon, and then without saying anything to my aunt, I got on my coat and went outside.

It had been rainy and dreary all week, but today it was fresh, warm, and sunny. I felt better the minute I hit the street. Nothing had changed. Same after-school noises and excitement. Same little kids jumping double-Dutch on the sidewalk, and a drug addict looking stupid and evil leaning in the doorway across the street. Same little boys trying to be tough, and grandmas on their way to shop. There was loud music from somebody's apartment, and I started tapping my foot to the beat. I hadn't heard that beat, my music, since last summer. I had forgotten how much I missed it. Same old street, same sounds, same looks, same music. It had been a long time.

"Is that you, Nia Jones?" said Mrs. Hartford who

lives in the apartment house across the street. "What are you doing home?"

"Oh, we're on break," I lied, quickly. Mrs. Hartford was the block gossip. I didn't feel like having my business all over the street before lunch.

"Hey, Nia!" a couple of the kids yelled as I went past.

"Hey!" I said back.

"Good morning!" Lin Wan said, peeking out from the counter in his shop.

"Hello," I said.

Damon, this kid I knew from first grade, nodded at me as I walked past, and I nodded back. He was standing in the spot where dope dealers stand. I wondered if he was starting to deal. I didn't say anything to him. He had that look.

Almost everybody on my block, except for a couple of losers, is real nice and knows everybody else. It made me feel good. It was good to be home.

"Nia! Nia!" I looked around and saw Wanda, this six-year-old who lives down the street and goes to my aunt's church. I've known her since she was born, she's like a little sister. She's real cute with Afro puffs her mama ties with red ribbons. Ever since I've known her she's always worn red ribbons. Even when she was a baby.

"You're back! You're back!" She gave me a big hug around the waist. I hugged her back. "Can you take me to Willowbrook Mall? My mommy said if I could find somebody to take me, she'd give them money for the bus and to buy some fries and a Coke at the McDonald's."

I laughed. I wasn't back fifteen minutes before Wanda was asking me to take her somewhere. Nothing had changed. "Okay," I said. She ran in to tell her mother.

"What are you doing back so early?" her mother yelled from the window.

"Break," I said.

"They let you-all out a lot in those white schools, don't they?"

I shrugged, not saying anything.

"Thanks. Nia, pick Wanda up some socks and a pink blouse at the Bamberger's. Wanda has the money. If you-all hurry you can catch the bus, it's due downtown in about half an hour." She closed the window just as Wanda bounced onto the sidewalk, and we started down the street.

Wanda's a good dancer, and she showed me a couple of new moves as we walked along, filling me in on everything that happened on the block since I'd been away. Who was seeing who; who was having a baby; who was getting married, and everything else. I was glad I hadn't told Mrs. Hartford any of my business; Wanda would be talking about *me* next time somebody asked. We caught the corner bus down to the transfer point and waited for the number 11 to the mall.

As we settled into our seats in the back of the bus, Rashida, this girl who used to go to my old school, and Rashid, her twin brother, got on. They were with this guy with about five pounds of gold chains around his neck, which was strange because gold's been played — nobody's wearing it anymore. But he was the kind of guy you'd be afraid to tell that to. When they saw me, they waved and came back to join us.

Rashida's not all that cute or nice, but she's always with cute boys because of Rashid. I guess having a twin brother can be almost as good as having a great personality. I hadn't seen Rashid for about two years, and he was looking good. He'd gotten real tall, and I hardly recognized him.

I was nervous for a minute and my lips started acting up like they do when I'm around cute boys, but then I remembered the time the Easter Bunny scared Rashid in Mrs. Perry's class in the first grade. The vice-principal came in dressed as the Easter Bunny to give out Easter eggs. Everybody knew who it was — you don't run into a lot of Easter Bunnies who smell like cigars — but everybody was cool, except Rashid. He carried on like a fool — even for somebody who was in the first grade. He cried, and bawled, and threw a natural fit until they finally had to call his mama to come from work and take him home. Everybody said that that was the last time somebody dressed up like the Easter Bunny and visited the first grade. Rashid had, single-handedly, changed all that. Remembering it, I smiled. Rashid looked at me a little strange, but he smiled back.

"Do I know you from somewhere?" he asked, trying to be cool.

"Weren't you in Mrs. Perry's class?" I asked. A shadow flitted across his eyes, which told me he probably remembered the Easter Bunny. I didn't push it.

"You-all *know* you know each other," Rashida

broke in. "Don't be acting cute! Nia, this is Darnell," she said, nodding toward Mr. Gold Chains. I nodded at Darnell and he nodded back. I wasn't sure Darnell could talk at first. He was real big and husky and when he opened his mouth to yawn, I'd never seen so many gold teeth in my life. His hands were as big as Wanda's face. But his eyes said everything. They didn't have any light in them. They looked mean, real mean.

"Where you been, Nia? I haven't seen you in a long time," Rashida asked.

"Well, last summer I took these classes over at Essex County, and then I was in school," I said. I avoid telling people I go away to boarding school, and I never mention Endicott if I can help it. I don't like them to think I'm showing off, like I think I'm better or smarter than them.

"So where do you go, to the Annex?" asked Rashid in a teasing voice. "You ain't been in school or I'd remember it." The Annex is the school where they send kids when they can't keep them in regular schools; tough kids, tackheads, kids who have been in juvenile detention and places like that. I knew Rashid was joking, and that he really didn't think I went to the Annex. If he had, he wouldn't be teasing me — some of those girls are *too* hard. Claiming the Annex was probably cooler than saying Endicott Academy, but then I checked out Darnell, sitting across the aisle, leaning like a gangster, looking like he could be *king* of the Annex.

"I used to go to this school but . . . I got thrown out for a couple of weeks and I've chosen not to go back," I said, as much to Hagen as to anybody else.

"Wow . . ." Rashid and Rashida said in unison. "Thrown out?"

Darnell leaned over and looked at me with new respect.

"You got thrown out of Endicott?" Wanda said with alarm. "Did you tell your aunt?"

I'd forgotten Wanda was sitting there, taking everything in, and for a minute I felt as ashamed as I'd felt that morning — but just as I was getting ready to say something to her, fate walked through the door of the bus. There I was, on my way to the mall, fooling around with Rashid, and who should get on the bus but Lucinda Spinotta.

I didn't recognize her at first. She was dressed in jeans the same as me, but she looked different. She had a couple of earrings in her ears (I had never noticed that she had pierced ears), and her hair was all over her head in some weird punk style. She was with some kids who looked kind of dangerous — the kind that trash a school or somebody's car. In fact, Lucinda looked like she could be riding on the back of a motorcycle throwing firebombs. She didn't look like herself, and she wasn't acting like herself, either.

We spotted each other at the same minute. She stared at me long and hard, too. She was with two big, tough-looking dudes and another girl who looked like she was her sister. The four of them headed to the back of the bus where we were sitting. Everyone got quiet, waiting for them to pass. I didn't tell my friends that I knew her, and she didn't say anything to her friends, either. It was like we were strangers. I searched her face for some sign of recognition. It glimmered there for a minute in her eyes, but then she snuffed it out — the same way I did. But her ignoring me — and my ignoring her — was different from the way it used to be at Endicott.

Darnell, who was sitting across from me with his legs swung over the aisle like he owned it, gave the guy with Lucinda a real mean look, but this guy looked just as mean as Darnell.

"Move your feet, dude," he said to Darnell.

"Tony," I heard Lucinda say to the guy. "Let's sit in the front." Darnell just kept looking at Tony like he didn't hear him.

"I said move your feet, dude," Tony said.

Tony was tall and big and looked like he spent his weekends hauling furniture up apartment stairs — the kind of guy you wouldn't want to tangle with. He had a cross around his neck and long hair that came to his shoulders.

"Step over them, dude," Darnell said, muttering the first words I'd heard from him. Rashid stiffened, glanced at Darnell, and then began sizing up the guy *with* Tony, who was sizing him up at the same time.

I felt Wanda tense up beside me. There was going to be a fight, I could smell it.

I looked at Lucinda who was standing behind Tony. She looked as pale as a ghost. She was scared, too.

Darnell got up to face Tony and the two of them stood there for a minute, not saying anything. Everybody on the bus got quiet. The bus driver peered back, watching them nervously. For the first time I noticed a bulge in Darnell's jacket. Something told me it was a gun. A lot of kids carry guns, and Darnell was definitely the kind of guy who would be strapped. He gave Rashid a little nod, as if to say, I got it covered, man, but Rashid looked as scared as me. Tony's friend looked like he might have some heat on him, too.

God, I thought to myself, What if they fight right here on the bus? What if there's a shoot-out? Wanda moved closer to me. I took her hand and hoped she couldn't tell mine was shaking.

"What did you say to me, nigger?" Tony asked.

"I said step over them, white boy, before I kick your white butt. You don't belong in this city, so get out of my town," replied Darnell.

"You people make me sick," Tony said.

"You people . . ." The scene was familiar except the actors were different, and my eye caught Lucinda's. We seemed to be communicating without saying anything. To this day, I don't know what it was: if we'd both figured that we'd had enough with this race mess and all that. If we were both just tired of it all. I knew I was scared, scared that Darnell or Tony was going to pull out a gun and blow somebody away. I guess we both knew we had to do something to stop it. We said it with our eyes. We moved at the same time.

She leaned over and whispered something to Tony, putting her hand on his. He paused, then glanced at her with a crooked smile, disdainful interest, then annoyance; then he looked straight ahead, dead at Darnell. I went into action.

"Were you in Mrs. Perry's class, too?" I said to Darnell, who was standing tough. It was the dumbest thing that anyone could say, considering the circumstances. I knew it and he knew it, too, but it was the only thing I could think of. He looked at me like I had lost my mind.

"What did you say, girl?" he asked, his eyes leaving Tony for a moment to look at me in disbelief. "What did you say?"

I glanced at him with a simple smile and repeated my inane question. "Were you in Mrs. Perry's class, too?"

Everybody, even Wanda, turned to look at me. Here I was, in the middle of a fight getting ready to start, talking about nothing — and talking loud, too, so everybody could hear me.

"I always liked fingerpainting," I said. Even the white guys were looking at me in amazement now. "But then I guess playing with clay was all right, too. I never liked Play-Doh that much, it always got under my nails."

Darnell looked at me and shook his head. "This girl's a fool," he said to nobody in particular. "This girl is out of her mind." Everybody started to laugh — except me and Lucinda. Fools have a way of transcending color.

Rashid looked pained, like he was ashamed to know me. I didn't blame him. I was ashamed to know me, too, but I didn't want there to be a fight. I guess Lucinda felt the same thing, because she started whispering like mad to Tony. Then she kissed him smack on the lips.

He looked as surprised as everybody else. He turned around, relaxed, and kissed her again. She drew back and gave him this phony smile. I had to hand it to the girl. I don't think I would have gone that far, kissing Darnell, to stop the fight. Making a fool of myself was about my limit.

Tony turned to her and grinned this grin that made my skin crawl, and they got off the bus. But Darnell and Tony hadn't fought. I guess we'd won.

Darnell went into this thing about white people after they'd gotten off the bus. Rashid and Rashida chimed in. I even put in my two cents' worth. I knew it wasn't the truth, but I said it anyway.

As I was getting off the bus, I heard Darnell saying something mean about me as the door was closing, but I didn't care.

I was glad to leave and go into the mall with Wanda. But I was still shaking. Color, money, anger. It seemed you couldn't get beyond those things no matter where you went — Endicott, Newark, or the 11 bus.

CHAPTER SEVEN

Wanda and I didn't say much as we walked into the mall. I guess she wanted to forget what had gone down on the bus as much as I did. She held my hand tight and wouldn't let it go for a long time. We started wandering in and out of stores, halfway looking for the stuff her mother had asked me to buy, and halfway just looking. After we'd bought everything we were supposed to buy, we walked over to where all the eating places were. It was a toss-up between McDonald's and Burger King. We settled on McDonald's — Wanda said the fries were better.

It seemed like everybody in the mall had gotten hungry the same minute we did, and everybody seemed to be getting into the same line. A huge guy with a checkered shirt barely pulled over his big belly nearly knocked Wanda out of line getting in front of her. I realized we didn't have that much money to spend. The blouse and socks had come to a lot more than Wanda's mama thought they would, so we were down to a dollar and a couple of quarters apiece.

"Let's go to Captain McKnight's," Wanda said, pointing to a fast-food restaurant wedged between McDonald's and Burger King. I'd never heard of the place, but Wanda seemed to know what she was talking about.

"The food is cheap there, and we can get more than we can get at other places."

"Is it good?" I asked.

"Kind of," she said doubtfully. "But you get two times more fries than you get at McDonald's, and it costs the same."

That was enough for me. We headed over to Captain McKnight's.

The minute we walked in, I knew we'd made a mistake. It was a dump. There were french fry containers on the floor, and the tables looked like they hadn't been washed off since that morning. There was a crack in the counter, and the napkin dispenser was broken. Napkins — some clean, some dirty — covered the floor like confetti. There were only two people working behind the counter: the person who took the orders and a girl who seemed to be doing all the cooking.

I was just about to tell Wanda that we were going to take our chances at one of the other places, when the girl turned around. I gasped in surprise. It was my girl Malika, and she was working hard.

She was shaking potatoes that were deep frying in a large pan with one hand, and turning burgers with the other. Every few minutes she would turn to the person at the counter who was taking the orders, and then leave everything to dash to the back of the store and check on something else. Her glasses were so steamed up you couldn't see her eyes. Sweat was pouring down her face. A little sailor cap with *Captain McKnight's* stitched across the top was sitting crookedly on top of her head, and the blouse and skirt that were supposed to look like a sailor's uniform had mustard and ketchup spilled in a weird design across the front. She looked a mess.

"Malika!" I screamed. "Malika!" Everybody in the place turned around to look at me.

"Nia!" she screamed back, and she started to come from behind the counter, but the person who was taking the orders gave her an evil look, and Malika stayed where she was. But as soon as the woman turned her back Malika stuck out her tongue. Wanda started giggling.

"May I help you, miss?" the woman who was taking the orders asked.

"Well . . ." I didn't say anything for a minute. I didn't like the way she had looked at Malika. I felt like sticking my tongue out, too.

"Yes?" she asked again impatiently.

"Two large fries and two large Cokes," Wanda chirped up before I could say anything.

"Two large fries and two large Cokes," the woman said to Malika, who without looking up started to fill our orders in double time.

I looked over the woman's shoulder at Malika who was holding up ten fingers and grimacing — like she was being held prisoner and trying to give me a message.

"Wait, wait," she mouthed slowly, then held up ten fingers again. I realized she was telling me to wait ten minutes for her. Wanda and I took our order and sat down to wait, munching our fries slowly.

Finally Malika rushed out carrying a Coke, almost spilling it as she gave me a hug. She'd been down South with her mom most of the summer, and when she'd gotten home, I'd been taking that class at Essex County College so I'd hardly seen her during the summer. I'd left for Endicott in August. We hugged each other so tightly neither of us could breathe for a minute.

"Nia," she said, "what are you doing home?" In the same breath she murmured as she nodded toward the woman behind the counter, "Let's move to another table." She gestured toward one that was on the far side of the room.

As Malika sipped her Coke, words poured out of her so fast I could hardly follow what she was saying.

"What you doing home from Endicott? God, I hate this place! How's your french fries? Don't tell anybody but I saw the cook who was here before me picking his nose while he was frying them! But don't worry, I fried yours so they're cool. God, I hate this place! What you doing in the mall? What you buy? I can't stand my boss, I wish she would drop dead in the frying oil! They actually make you pay for your own lunch. God . . ."

"Why are you working here?" I finally asked, forcing a word in edgewise. Wanda and I had both lost our appetite for the fries the minute Malika'd mentioned the nasty habits of the cook. We'd both pushed our potatoes over to the far side of our plates.

Malika slammed her Coke down on the counter and gave me a puzzled look. "You been going to that rich white school so long you forget how the other half lives," she said with a laugh.

"Ummph!" Wanda said. "She really dissed you!"

"Why do you *think* I'm working in a crummy place like this?" she asked, narrowing her eyes. "I need the money, that's why."

Nobody said anything for a few minutes. I stared at the salt and pepper shakers. Wanda slurped her soda. Malika started eating the ice in the bottom of her glass.

"I've got to make some money," she said softly. "So what you doing home anyway?" she asked again.

I paused for a moment, trying to figure out what to do with Wanda while I talked to Malika. Wanda's eyes had focused on a spot on the ceiling and she looked like she wasn't paying attention — a clear sign that she would listen with all ears to every word I would say. Wanda had already heard more about my business then I wanted her to hear. I didn't want her to know the gory details. I spotted a video machine in the corner, so I gave her a couple of quarters and told her to go play it.

"I got kicked out for two weeks," I said as soon as she was out of earshot. Malika looked at me and shook her head.

"Kicked out?" she asked. "Who you trying to be? Debra?"

That crack surprised me, but I didn't pick up on it. I told her what had happened at Endicott with Marcus and Lucinda and all. I even told her about what had happened on the bus.

"Damn!" she said after I'd finished. "It's a good thing that Tony guy and Darnell didn't mix it up. I would have been seeing you-all on the ten o'clock news." She sipped her soda thoughtfully, making a slurping sound as she sucked up the last bit from the bottom of the paper cup. "So this was all over that dude you been talking about for the past two years?"

"Yeah."

"You got expelled from Endicott over a man?" she said finally, the disappointment clearly written on her face.

"It wasn't over a man — it was over principles."

"So are you going back?"

"I've chosen not to go back," I said. I couldn't seem to get the way Hagen had said those words out of mind. Malika looked at me like I was crazy.

"Well, girlfriend, you've *chosen* to be a fool," she said. "You've *chosen* principles over reality, and principles and two dollars will get you a greasy burger and some nasty fries at this place."

I looked at her in surprise. "It meant something to me," I said.

"You're throwing away everything over doodoo," Malika said back.

"Don't be so hard," I said, trying to sound casual, but I was getting mad. I felt like I was talking to Aunt Odessa, and I was wishing I'd lied about Endicott the way I'd started to.

We sat there in silence. The same song kept playing again and again over the loudspeaker. I glanced at Malika. Her skin used to be so smooth. My aunt used to say that she looked like she belonged in a Dove commercial. But now there were tiny pimples on her forehead and across her nose. I wondered if all the grease from doing all that frying was making her break out. She looked tired, and in a strange kind of way she looked older.

"I wish I'd had the chance you had," she said after a minute, more to herself than to me. "I wish I could have gone there."

I suddenly remembered that Malika had had the chance to go away to school, too, but her mom hadn't let her go.

Malika's mom belongs to this church — Aunt Odessa calls it a cult — that makes her do all kinds of weird things. She's always wearing long dresses; she can't eat certain foods on certain days; and she can't "commune with those who have traffic with the devil," who are, according to her leader, almost everybody who doesn't belong to the group. She didn't make Malika go to church with her, but she had to follow some of the rules. She'd even made Malika turn down the scholarship to a good school because she felt that the people there "trafficked with the devil."

"Endicott is not what you think," I said. "It looks

good on paper, but it's really a lot of bull when you get there. A lot of kids don't really fit in — like me. Believe me, you wouldn't have, either. You would have hated it the same way I did."

"I don't fit in here," Malika said, looking me straight in the eye.

"What do you mean?" I asked her.

"My mom has *truly* started to get on my nerves," she said after a minute.

I breathed a sigh of relief. Her mom had always gotten on her nerves. Her mom got on *my* nerves.

"So what else is new?" I asked. "I don't mean to dis your mama, but she gets on everybody's nerves with that 'trafficking with the devil' mess."

"That's not the only thing," Malika said with annoyance. "This stupid job. The school I go to. It's not the way it was before."

"School?" I asked. "Malika, you are school's mama! The original straight-A kid. How could *you* be sick of school?"

"The school I go to is not Endicott Academy, Nia," she snapped. "It's boring and dumb. I'm scared half the time, because some of the guys carry knives and they even found a gun on one kid. A lot of the teachers are as scared as the kids. It's not like junior high, Nia."

"But you're smart."

"Right. Most of the so-called smart kids don't have moms like mine who are scared of finding the devil under every traffic light. They've got people behind them, people in their corner who are going to see that they make it no matter what. People like your aunt. I've only got myself. I have to make it on my own."

"But, Malika, you're making some money, at least you've got — "

"I know you're not going to mention this job. I know you're not that stupid!" Malika paused for a minute, catching her breath. "I thought slavery was dead until I started working for these people. I get $4.75 an hour. It costs me two dollars a day to get out here and back and they make us pay for our own lunch. And they expect us to *eat* here! They're crazy." She stopped suddenly, looked around, and I followed her eyes. The cashier was glaring at her from across the room.

"In case you haven't figured out who that ugly witch is throwing us the evil eye, she's my boss," Malika said as she chomped on some more ice. "In a minute she's going to nod her head and let me know it's time to get back to work."

"Why don't you just quit?"

"Right, Nia. Quit? Do you know how hard it is for a kid in high school to get a job? People your aunt's age who have been working for centuries are taking jobs like this. I looked everywhere, *everywhere* — McDonald's, Burger King, Kentucky Fried Chicken, Dunkin' Donuts — you think I'd be working in this zoo if I could have got a job at a decent place?

"It's on me, Nia. On me. If I'm going to get to college I've got to make the money myself. Yeah, I might be able to score some money somewhere, but it will be a drop in the bucket. It won't pay for everything. I've looked in catalogs, and I've talked to people, and the schools I want to go to cost as much as my mom makes in a year! And my SAT scores have got to be smoking. I know I'm smart, and I know I could beat any of these rich kids who are going to be applying to the same schools as me if I had a decent chance. But my school doesn't have the money other schools have. The encyclopedias in the library are five years old."

"But at least you're here," I said finally. "You're at home. At least you and Debra can party, hang out, do the stuff we used to do."

"The only thing I do is study hard and try to stay on the honor roll so somebody will give me some money to get into college. I don't have time to party. All I have time to do is work and go to school." Malika leaned over toward me like she was going to tell me a secret, but she didn't whisper it. "And as for Debra . . . even if I had the time, I wouldn't party with Debra and her *new friends.*"

I wondered what she was talking about, but before I could say anything her boss gave her that nod she'd been talking about.

"Break's up!" Malika said with a toss of her head. "Back to the plantation." She gathered up the stuff on the table and piled it onto one tray. Then she went to the next table and piled more stuff on. Then she went to a third and piled on still more. She held the top of one cup with her chin as she slowly made it to the trash can with her pile of trash. But she lifted her chin a bit so that she could talk as she passed back by our table. I guess I must have been looking pretty down because she gave me a smile.

"Hey," she said. "I *know* that no matter what it takes, I'm going to make it. I don't throw good luck that comes *my* way out the door. But you, sister-lady, you better check yourself out." She made it to the nearest trash can and dumped everything into it without looking back.

CHAPTER EIGHT

I thought about what Malika had said all the way home. I wished I could forget the look on her face, but I couldn't. As I opened the door of my apartment and stepped into the kitchen, the last thing I was thinking about was my aunt.

I had forgotten that I had left without telling Aunt Odessa I was going out. But she hadn't forgotten. She was sitting at the table smoking a cigarette, something I hate to see her do. Smoke was drifting up and curling around her hair. She was cooking something on the stove, and smoke was curling up from that, too. She was mad. I was mad about what Malika had said to me. Even the people on TV looked mad. The moment I caught Aunt Odessa's eye, I felt like heading back to the mall, but it was too late. She started in on me again before I could even take off my coat.

"Just what is wrong with you, young lady?" she

asked, her eyebrows screwed up into a scowl. "You sneak out of here without telling me where you're going. You fight, fight like some street girl and get thrown out of one of the best prep schools in the country. After I had to scrape and steal and beg to get you in. You . . ."

She was starting in on Endicott again, and I didn't feel like hearing it, so I didn't give her a chance to finish.

"No one told you to beg or scrape to get me into that stupid place. I didn't even want to go to that dumb school. That's on you, not me," I said.

"Just what did you think you were going to do?" she asked. "Did you plan to go to this high school here with the thugs from this street? You going to start carrying on with Damon, that little crackhead dealer out there standing on the sidewalk? What do you plan to do, missy, just tell me that."

That "missy" business always plucks it for me, and she knows it. I hate to fight with Aunt Odessa, but I knew a fight was coming. I fixed my mouth in a straight line determined not to say anything else. It didn't matter.

"And just where *were* you this afternoon?" she asked, getting back to that.

"I went to the mall," I said. "I took Wanda, her mother asked me to."

"You didn't ask me if you could go," she said.

"You were so busy yelling at me, even if I'd asked you, you wouldn't have heard me," I said without missing a beat.

"Don't get fresh with me!"

"I'm not getting fresh with you, I'm just telling you the truth."

"One of the best prep schools in the country, *the* best prep school in the country," she muttered, starting in on that again.

I let out a sigh; unfortunately, it sounded like a yawn. Aunt Odessa looked at me with rage in her eyes. "Don't you yawn in my face, young lady," she snapped. "You can just thank God they didn't throw you out permanently. Thank God you can go back. Thank God you'll have another chance. Thank God — "

"You can thank God, all you want to, but I'm not going back," I said and closed my mouth — shocked at how my own voice sounded. But I didn't care.

"What did you say?"

"I said I'm not going back."

"What are you talking about, of course you're going back."

"I'm not going back," I said again. "And you can't make me. I want to go to the high school here like everybody else does," I said. "I want to be like the rest of my friends." I kind of hesitated when I said friends — I wasn't sure if I could really consider Malika a friend; she'd really been down on me. But I knew that Debra was still my girl.

"You don't know what you're talking about!" Aunt Odessa said. "You better start talking some sense."

"I *am* talking sense," I said and I really meant it.

"You'll do what I tell you to do," Aunt Odessa said. Her face was tense and so tight I could see the lines around her mouth.

"I'll do whatever the hell I feel like doing," I shouted.

I don't know why I said that. The words just seemed to come from nowhere. Aunt Odessa banged her hand down on the table so hard I could almost feel it. She rose from her seat and glared at me as if I were some undesirable form of life, and her eyes could have froze the place I'd just mentioned.

"What did you say to me?" she screamed. "What did you say to me?"

I guess one of my problems is I don't know how to be cool, how to cut my losses, leave the game while I still have some dignity. In other words, I don't know when to shut up.

"You don't need to scream at me, I can hear. I'm not deaf!" I yelled back at her. And I turned to go into my room. But then she hit me below the belt — way below the belt.

"What would your parents say if they could see you now," she hissed. "If Bernard and Laura could hear you talking to me like you're talking to me. If they could hear you curse at me. If they knew you had been thrown out of school like this! They'd be so ashamed of you!"

I stopped and turned to stare at her, and at that moment I hated Aunt Odessa. I hated her because there was no way I could answer that.

"I hate you for bringing my parents into it," I said.

"I hate you for trying to turn them against me all because of that stupid, dumb school. I hate you!" I screamed at the top of my lungs and I started to cry as I went into my room and slammed the door behind me.

I knew I wasn't making any sense. I knew she couldn't turn my parents against me — they were dead — but I hated her bringing up their memory like that, shaming me. I sat down on my bed and picked up Dandelion. He comes in handy at times like these. I held him tight, squeezing him against my breast. Some more of his stuffing came out, so I unhooked one of the safety pins that hold him together, pushed his stuffing back inside, and fastened him up again. I settled back on my bed with my head propped against the wall. I'd stopped crying, but I was still sobbing inside.

I think about my parents often. When I do it's like they're characters in a fairy tale or something — good angels who watch over me. Even though I was a baby when they died, I feel like I know them in some way. I have their pictures, their wedding picture and the special one — the one taken with me. It was taken a few months before they were killed. I'm wrapped in a pink crocheted blanket Aunt Odessa made for me, and my mother is holding me. My mom and dad are both smiling so hard you've got to smile, too, when you look at them.

They look real young in the picture. They had me when they were both nineteen, and I look almost as old as them now even though I'm just fifteen. When

I was little they seemed so big in that picture, but the older I get the younger they look. They're almost beginning to look like my brother and sister. I've caught up to them. I guess maybe someday they'll even look like my kids.

What *would* my parents say? I wondered.

The telephone rang, and I picked it up at the same time my aunt did in the kitchen.

"Hello," I said into the receiver. My aunt banged down the other end.

"Baby, baby, Rashida called and told me she saw you on the bus this afternoon, but I didn't believe her. Welcome home!" said a deep voice on the other end of the line. There was nobody in the world who had a voice like that except Debra. My aunt used to say that Debra's voice was too old to belong to a kid. It was raspy and sexy, the kind of voice you associate with some sophisticated model selling perfume on TV.

"Debra!" I screamed into the phone. "Debra! Its so good to hear your voice." And I was telling the truth. There was nobody in this world I could think of at that moment that I wanted to talk to more. We both started giggling at the same time, the same as we always did. It was like coming home, finally.

"What's been going on? I saw Malika today in the mall," I said. There was a pause on the other end — not a long pause, just for a few seconds, like Debra was catching her breath.

"Me and Malika, we don't hang together too tough anymore," she said after a minute. I didn't say anything. If Malika acted as snippy with Debra as she had with me I could certainly understand why. "So you going to be here for a while or you going back to that ritzy school?"

I laughed. "I'm going to be here a while," I said. I didn't want to say too much about Endicott. I was sick of talking about it.

"Well, are you up to hanging out?" she asked. I paused for a minute, not sure what she meant by hanging out.

"Are you up for going out tonight?" she asked, not waiting for me to answer. "Come on, it's early. It's only eight."

Aunt Odessa was already mad at me. I knew she wouldn't let me go out again. But Debra *did* live across the street. Maybe if I apologized about what I'd said this afternoon, she might let me go. I decided it would be worth a try.

"Tell her you're coming over to help me watch Tina," Debra said. "Tell her I'm home alone and I'm scared." Tina was Debra's little sister, and in the old days the three of us — me, Malika, and Debra — would baby-sit together. I was surprised how quickly Debra could come up with a lie for me.

"Okay," I said.

"She'll let you do it," Debra said, sure of herself. "I'll meet you outside my place. Ring the doorbell — one time long and once short — and I'll come downstairs."

"But what about Tina?" I asked, but Debra had hung up.

I went into the kitchen. My aunt was reading the newspaper.

"Aunt Odessa?" I asked. She didn't say anything. "Aunt Odessa, I'm sorry about this afternoon." I paused for a minute. Aunt Odessa looked up over the newspaper. I could tell she was still mad. "I'm really sorry. I really am," I said, trying to sound contrite. I tried to put a little catch in my voice to make it sound like I was on the verge of crying. My aunt rolled her eyes; she knew the catch was fake. She ignored me and went back to reading her newspaper. "Aunt Odessa," I said again. "That was Debra on the phone. She's home alone with Tina and said she was scared. She asked if I could come over for a while to keep her company. I promise I'll be back before eleven."

"What's she got to be scared of?" Aunt Odessa asked me, looking me straight in the eye. "Tough as *she* is, folks should be scared of her."

I shrugged my shoulders. "I don't know," I said. "Please let me go. I just . . . I just need to talk to one of my friends." That was the truth. Aunt Odessa looked at me again and then glanced back at her paper.

"I shouldn't let you go anywhere," she muttered under her breath, and my heart sank. "But if you're just going across the street, I guess it will be all right. Just behave yourself and be back by midnight."

"Thanks," I said quickly. And I headed toward the door as fast as I could go before she could change her mind.

CHAPTER NINE

I rang the doorbell twice — one time long and once short like Debra had told me to do. I could hear her high-heels clicking down the hall and stairs as she came to meet me.

"What's up?" she asked as she stepped outside. Then she turned and gave me a mysterious smile with a look that said "hi" and "check me out" all at the same time. When I did, my breath almost left my body. From her Gucci bag and shoes to her big gold earrings to her tight, short, black leather skirt, she was not the Debra I remembered. Her "hair" — or should I say weave — was falling down around her shoulders, and she kept flipping it up and around in a way that would have made Charlotte envious — except Charlotte's hair was real. Debra's nails were so red and long they looked like lethal weapons. But her eyes topped it all off — they were hazel! Debra had bought herself a new pair of eyes! I couldn't stop looking at them; they reminded me of the eyes zombies have in movies.

"Debra?!" I gasped and asked at the same time.

She pulled me close to her and smacked a kiss on the side of my face. I could smell the sweet scent of Juicy Fruit gum mingled with Obsession cologne as she pulled away. She winked a slow seductive wink, showing off her new eyes.

"Like 'em? They look good, don't they!" she said before I could disagree. "So you ready to go?" she asked. I didn't say anything; I still wasn't sure where we were going. I glanced up toward my building, making sure my aunt hadn't decided to look out of the window. The blind was still down.

"Where are we going? Can we talk inside?" I asked. I didn't want to press my luck.

"Still scared of Odessa, huh?" Debra said with a kind of patronizing chuckle. My aunt had always told me that Debra had a know-it-all attitude, but it never really bothered me. Debra *did* know it all most of the time.

"I'm not scared of my aunt," I said weakly. "I just don't want to be standing around out here with nothing to do."

"We *have* something to do," Debra said mysteriously. "I beeped Johnny right after you called, and he'll be meeting us here in a few minutes." She stood back and gave me an appraising glance. "I guess you look all right for where we're going."

"Where *are* we going?" I asked again. "And who is Johnny?"

"We're going to Boomerangs, that club on Central

Avenue. Johnny is Johnny Lincoln. We been going together since the middle of August."

"Johnny Lincoln!!" I screeched. I couldn't believe it. Johnny Lincoln was one of the biggest sleaze bags on the block. He was around twenty-four years old, and the kind of dude my aunt would suck her teeth at when she'd see him cross the street, and shake her head at when he'd turn the next corner. Before I went to Endicott, the three of us — me, Debra, and Malika (when it had really been the three of us) would crack on him and his bald-headed self all the time. Whenever we saw him, Malika would make a cross with her forefingers like they do in old vampire movies. He was definitely a blood-sucking kind of guy. A lot of people said he was a dope dealer. And what kind of a twenty-four-year-old man would go out with a sixteen-year-old kid?

"Johnny Lincoln!! Why are you going out with Johnny Lincoln?" I asked increduously. Debra avoided my eyes. "And why is he taking us to Boomerangs! Debra, I don't want to go to Boomerangs! Especially with . . ." But before I could get his name out of my mouth, Johnny Lincoln drove up in a red Maxima trimmed in gold. And before I knew it, I was being shoved into the backseat by Debra.

The smell of cigarettes and lemony cologne filled my nose as the car door slammed behind me like the door to a funeral vault in a horror movie. I felt slightly dizzy but strangely alert all at the same time. I found myself smiling a fake smile and looking at myself like I was watching a movie.

"Johnny, this is my girlfriend, Nia," Debra said as

she settled into the backseat beside me. She squeezed my arm hard, like a cross mother does to a kid in a supermarket so he won't embarrass her by making a scene.

I threw her a dirty look.

"Just be cool. We'll be back before eleven. You can call your aunt from the club. She won't know where you're calling from," Debra whispered in my ear. "Please, Nia," she added. Something about the way she said "please" told me that a lot was riding on my being cool, so I closed my mouth, leaned back in the seat, and prayed my aunt hadn't decided to open the window to get some fresh air.

"What'd you say your name was?" Johnny Lincoln asked, turning to check me out as he pulled away from the curb.

"Nia," I said, trying to be cool like Debra had told me to be.

If it hadn't been for the gold earrings that shone from his ears and his shiny bald head that gleamed like it had been waxed, you might have been able to say that Johnny Lincoln was handsome. As I examined his face, I tried to imagine what Debra saw in him. There was kind of a cool, dangerous air about him, but it was more scary than attractive.

"What'd she say?" the man who was sitting in the front seat beside Johnny asked, and my attention turned to him. He was shorter than Johnny and his head barely cleared the seat. I hadn't noticed him when I'd climbed in.

"Nia," I said again. He was dressed like Johnny, in a black leather jacket and pants that matched, except that he wore a shirt that he'd opened, and he had on a thick gold chain like somebody in a 1970s disco film.

"She's kind of cute, Snake," he said. For a minute I thought there was somebody else in the car, and then I remembered that "Snake" was Johnny's nickname.

"Nia, meet Reed," Johnny aka Snake said.

"How old are you, girl? What'd you say your name was? Nina?" Reed asked.

"Nia," I said, finding my voice from somewhere. "I'm fifteen."

Reed said, lighting a cigarette, "That's jailbait, Snake. I don't mess with no jailbait."

Thank you, God, I said to myself. But the two of them hunched in the front seat scared me, and my heart was pounding in my chest.

As we pulled away from the curb, I glanced out the back window at my apartment building and a feeling of dread swept through me. Here I was sitting in a car that could be stolen for all I knew, going to a club that I wasn't supposed to go to, with two strange men who I wasn't even supposed to know. I was headed for trouble. I knew that if my aunt ever found out about any of this I would be dead meat. In the space of half an hour I was going to break two of my aunt's most sacred commandments: Never ride in a car with strange men. Never go to a club where alcohol is served.

I glanced at Debra, who had become Miss Cool.

"Relax, Nia," she whispered. "Everything will be fine."

I leaned back against the plush seat, took a deep breath, and tried to pretend I was somewhere else.

"Anybody want a forty?" Johnny Lincoln asked as he screwed the top off of a bottle of malt liquor with one hand. I cringed as I saw him take a sip. I hoped he wasn't going to drink enough to get himself drunk or arrested for drinking while driving. I could see my aunt coming down to the station — or morgue — to get me. He passed it back to Debra, who drank some and then passed it on to me.

"No thanks," I said, trying not to sound like a wimp.

I passed it on to Reed, who gave me a leering wink that made me want to throw up. Johnny Lincoln turned the volume of the radio up, and the bass was jumping. As we pulled up to Boomerangs I breathed a sigh of relief. At least we would be out of the car.

"We're here," Debra said cheerfully as she opened the door.

Boomerangs was dark and hot. The whole place was covered with mirrors — on the ceiling, on the walls, on the bar, on the ladies' room door. I like my music loud. My aunt always says she's afraid I'm going to go deaf or they're going to throw us out of the building. But this music was *loud*.

The bouncer was frisking everyone to make sure no one was strapped and was going to shoot everybody up. But when he got to us, Johnny gave him a nod.

They're with me, the nod said; we passed through as if we were visiting royalty. He didn't ask us for our IDs, either. A couple of kids who didn't have IDs flashed us jealous looks as we coasted past.

It was so dark I could barely see in front of me as we moved slowly to a table near the back of the club. Johnny gestured for us to sit down and then looked at Debra and nodded toward the bar.

"You want a Coke?" Debra asked me.

"Okay," I shouted over the din of the music.

Johnny nodded toward the bartender. He came over to the table and took our orders.

The music was too loud for us to talk, and nobody was talking to me anyway. Reed had gone to the bar and had his arm around a woman in a tight blouse and short shorts. Johnny had his arm around Debra and every now and then he would nibble on her neck. He really is a vampire, I thought to myself. The thought of it almost made me laugh, but I caught myself. When the waiter brought my Coke, I settled back and started to sip it. It dripped on the table, leaving water spots on my blouse as I put it to my lips.

As people came into the club, they'd look over at our table and wave. Johnny acknowledged their greetings with a nod. All he ever did was nod. His eyes looked almost empty. As I watched him, I realized that he *was* like a snake — slow, smooth, and cold-blooded.

Johnny seemed to know everybody, and everybody seemed to know Debra because she was with him. She looked at me from across the table and smiled. I tried to smile back. Johnny got up without saying anything and walked into another room with a man dressed all in white. Walking together, heads bowed as they talked, they looked like they'd just stepped out of some gangster movie. Debra scooted down next to me after he had left.

"Isn't he something?" she whispered in my ear, her voice full of pride.

"Yeah," I said sipping my Coke. "He is *definitely* something."

"What did you say?" she asked. Unless we shouted, we couldn't hear each other over the sound of the music. I nodded. "Yeah," I said.

"What . . . ?" she asked again.

"Can we go to the ladies' room and talk?" I asked as loudly as I could. I wanted to have a chance to at least talk to her before Johnny came back.

"What?" she asked over the music.

"Bathroom?" I said so loudly that a couple sitting next to us looked at me. Debra stood up, and I followed her to the back of the club.

The bathroom was as bright as the club was dark, and the fluorescent light shone on every slip of toilet paper on the floor and smudge of dirt on the walls. The toilets didn't have seats, and water dripped in the sink. But it was quieter than the club.

"Did you see how Johnny knows everybody?" Debra asked with a wide grin. She glanced at the broken mirror, opened her Gucci pocketbook, took out a tube of lipstick, and spread a red glossy line across her lips.

"Did you notice how good everybody treats him? How much everybody respects him?" she asked, not waiting for me to answer. "Did you see how they didn't even ask for our IDs because we were with him? He's got juice. And let me tell you something else." She drew me close to her. "He's got all kinds of contacts with a lot of the rap groups. You know, a couple of acts are from around here, and he's going to get me in some videos. He *promised* me that. Some *videos*!! Nia, that's what I want to do more than anything else."

"Videos?" I asked.

"I'm going to be a star! I'm going to be big-time, too." I looked at her face, wondering if she was joking, if she knew how corny that line sounded. But she had a starry-eyed look, like she really believed what she had said.

"We really didn't know him when we used to talk about him. He's nice to me," she said quickly, with a defensive shrug as if she could read my mind.

"Nice? What's nice?" I asked.

"He just does nice things for me."

"Like what?"

"Like he doesn't let anybody mess with me," she said, looking down at her hands. "He's going to get me in some videos like I just said. And he's said with my looks and the way I can dance, I'll go straight to the top. You'll be seeing me on TV, girlfriend. On TV!"

I looked, really looked, at Debra. I could still see one of my best friends through the hazel eyes and everything else. But I could also see a change. While Malika had seemed older, Debra seemed younger. Not as smart as she used to be. She should know that anybody who the world called Snake had to be just that. He would end up biting her.

"What about school?" I asked her. "If you're going to be in all the videos, how are you going to have time for school?" It seemed like a dumb question but I asked it anyway.

"School?" she asked. "You don't know about high school, Nia. It's bad, real bad. You been sitting around with all those rich white kids so long you don't know how it is to deal with some of the thugs in high shool. Sometimes I'm scared, the other kids are scared — the teacher's even scared. He'll try to pretend he's not, but when some of these guys come into class all late and stuff, he won't say anything to them. He just keeps from looking at them and he won't look at anybody else. Some of the guys have knives. But Johnny won't let anybody mess with me. Everybody knows that I'm his lady."

"It can't be that bad," I said. "Nothing could be bad enough for you to take up with Johnny Lincoln."

"You just don't understand, do you?" she asked, and there was surprise in her voice. "Johnny takes care of me. Everything I need, Johnny gets for me. He gives me money to get my hair done. He buys me things." She shoved her Gucci pocketbook in my direction and opened it wide for me to see inside. Everything — the wallet, sunglass case, change purse, makeup bag — had the Gucci emblem. Counting the pocketbook, she must have had $800 worth of Gucci stuff.

"Is it the real thing?" I asked as I dug into the pocketbook, pulled out the change purse, and fingered it like Midas fingering his gold.

"What do you think?" Debra said with a toss of her hair weave.

"He definitely buys you things," I agreed. I'd be lying if I didn't admit that I got a sudden, quick rush of admiration for Johnny. But it was quick. Real quick.

Debra must have noticed the look on my face. "You just don't understand," she said again. "You've lost track of what the real deal is like out here."

"I haven't lost track of anything," I said. "I haven't forgotten anything. I know a sleaze bag when I see one, and Johnny Lincoln is a sleaze bag . . . and I know what kind of girl goes with a sleaze bag like that."

Debra looked like she was going to slap my face, and then she looked real hurt and mad, and then like she was going to cry.

"I didn't mean that," I said quickly. Maybe she really liked him, I thought. Maybe there was more to him than I remembered. Maybe Endicott had blinded me to a lot of what was real in life. I went over to Debra and put my arms around her. She didn't pull away.

"I'm sorry," I said, and I really meant it.

We stood there for a minute or two in that nasty bathroom without saying anything else. A woman came in, went into one of the stalls, and flushed the toilet noisily. She came out, glanced at herself in the mirror, washed her hands, and left.

"So what are you doing home?" Debra asked. I guess she was tired of talking about Johnny. I was tired of talking about him, too. It was too depressing.

"I got kicked out for two weeks," I said. I didn't go into the whole story. Debra was so different, so changed, I knew somehow she really wouldn't care.

"So what did Odessa say?"

"You don't want to know," I said.

"What does your mom say about Johnny?" I asked.

"You don't want to know," Debra said, and we both started to laugh.

"You know what the real story is with your aunt?" Debra said finally.

"What?"

"You know she lives with that dude, you know, her boyfriend Winston, when you're not here, don't you?"

"What?" I finally sputtered. For a minute, I thought Debra was just trying to get even with me for saying those things about Johnny.

"You mean, you didn't know that?" she asked real serious, and I could tell by the tone of her voice that she just wasn't trying to be mean.

"No," I said.

"I'm sorry, I . . ."

"That's okay," I said. Somehow after tonight, nothing would surprise me.

"Come on," Debra said, with one last glance at the mirror. "Let's go catch up with Johnny and Reed." She glanced at her watch. It was solid gold, or at least it looked that way to me. "It's almost eleven. I'll tell Johnny to drive you home like I promised."

"Okay," I said.

We went back to the table and sat down. Johnny was nowhere to be seen. The bartender brought us another Coke. I looked at Debra's watch again; it was eleven-fifteen. At eleven-thirty, I started getting nervous. Finally Johnny came back to the table. He was looking more evil than he had when he left.

"Can we take Nia home?" Debra asked, sounding like a little girl.

"Do I look like a cab to you?" Johnny asked, his voice as cold as ice. Debra looked down at the table, her eyes shifting to avoid mine. I knew she was ashamed. My stomach dropped to my knees. What am I going to do? I wondered. I couldn't call anybody — there was nobody to call, and even if I'd had somebody to call I didn't have a quarter.

I didn't want it to get too late because I knew Aunt Odessa would phone Debra's house if I wasn't home soon. The very thought of what she would do to me when she found out I'd lied to her made my blood run cold. I started thinking furiously about something to tell her, but my mind was completely blank. I looked at Debra's watch again; it was eleven-forty-five. Midnight would be when Aunt Odessa would pick up that phone. If I could make it home before then, I'd probably be all right.

"Nia," Debra whispered in my ear. "Come on, I'm going to get you a cab."

"Debra, I don't — "

"Don't worry about it," Debra said. "I've got the money." We got up to head for the door.

"Where you think you're going?" Johnny Lincoln asked.

"I'm going to get my friend a cab home. That's all. I'm coming right back," Debra said, her voice small.

Johnny nodded, dismissing us, and picked up his drink. "Don't be too long," he said.

The air was cold and crisp as we stepped outside. It made me feel fresh and clean, almost like I'd taken a cool shower on a hot day. A group of cabs were parked about a block from the club, and as we headed toward them Debra handed me a twenty-dollar bill.

"This should cover it," she said.

"Debra," I said, turning to face her. "Please come home with me. Please."

"Can't do that," she said. "You heard Johnny. I've got to go back."

"He isn't your mother," I said, suddenly mad at Johnny Lincoln, at Debra, at everything. "You don't belong to him." But Debra was looking past me into the night.

"I just want to be somebody, to really make it big," she said. "And Johnny seems like the best way to do it."

As she was turning to leave, I grabbed her and gave her the hug of her life. She pulled back and smiled at me.

"What was that for?" she asked.

I shrugged. I really wasn't sure myself.

I made it home just as Aunt Odessa was picking up the phone to dial Debra's apartment. She looked at her watch as I closed the door behind me; I mumbled good night and ducked into my room before she could say anything.

As I sat down on my bed, I suddenly felt like crying, but no tears would come. I was scared for Debra. So much had changed in her life. But so much had changed in mine, too.

Endicott had only been the beginning. *Nothing* was like it had been. Not Debra, not Malika, and if my aunt was living with Winston, even she had changed. There really wasn't any space for me here anymore, either. I didn't belong anywhere. I lay on my bed being depressed for about an hour. It was probably two in the morning before I finally drifted off to sleep.

It seemed like only a few minutes had passed before I heard my aunt banging on my door. She didn't wait for me to tell her to come in.

I thought about asking her about Winston, but then I decided against it. She probably would have told me it was none of my business.

"Time for you to get up. You may be at home, but that's no excuse for laziness," she said as she lit up a cigarette. She knows I hate her to smoke in my room. I figured she was just doing it because she was still mad at me. I fanned the smoke away without saying anything. She ignored me. "I'm on the noon-to-midnight shift. As soon as you get up, report to me in the kitchen. I have some chores that I want done before I come home tonight."

I almost rolled my eyes when she said "report to me," but I didn't; I just glued them to the ceiling. As she turned to leave she tossed something on the bed. "By the way, this came for you in the mail," she said.

"Thanks," I said to the closing door. As I looked at the letter my heart skipped a beat and I let out a yell. Scribbled in the return address corner, in a familiar scrawl that I'd recognize anywhere in the world, were three words: *Marcus Garvey Williams.*

CHAPTER TEN

Dear Nia, Marcus's letter began. *I guess you're home for Thanksgiving break. I'm sending this now, in October, because I wanted to make sure you got the money before I spent it on something else. The money I make now goes into other things. I think about you a lot and I miss you and some of the other kids from Endicott. I'm sorry I couldn't tell you good-bye, but I had to get out fast. Please take care of yourself. I won't be in touch with you until I get control of my life. Marcus.*

That was all it said. I turned it over looking for some more and almost missed the $50 that fluttered onto my lap. I tucked the money into my pocket and read the letter again, and then glanced at the envelope for a return address. Nothing. Just his name.

Get control of his life. What had happened to him? *Money I make now goes into other things.* What other things? Drugs? The thought of it made me shiver.

I *had* to talk to him. I had to find out what was going on. Marcus Garvey Williams owed me. He owed me an explanation for what had happened. He owed me the same way I'd owed him when I'd given him Winston's fifty bucks.

I got out of bed and went over to the bag I'd brought back from Endicott, dumped it on the floor, and dug through it, looking for my address book with Marcus's New York telephone number. I tore it open to Marcus's name.

"Dumb! Dumb! Dumb!" I yelled angrily at myself when I found it. Last summer, when I'd been so mad at him, I'd scratched his number out in a rage when he hadn't returned my calls. I got a pencil and tried to erase the marks, but I couldn't do it without tearing the paper. "Damn!" I said out loud. Then I held it up to the light. I could just make the numbers out. I grabbed my phone and dialed them slowly.

It seemed like a hundred years before somebody answered on the other end.

"Hello," a woman said. The voice sounded tired, as if she had just got up. I glanced at the clock on my night table and realized that it was seven-thirty in the morning. She *was* just getting up.

"Is Marcus there?" I asked guiltily; it was too late to hang up. There was a long pause on the other end of the line.

"Who is this?" the voice angrily demanded.

She sounded so mad, for a minute I thought about

giving a false name, but I managed to squeak out my real one. "It's Nia Jones."

"Who?"

"Nia Jones, Mrs. Williams. I'm a friend of Marcus's from Endicott Academy." There was a long pause on the other end of the line, and I thought for a minute that she'd hung up. But then she answered and her voice sounded sad.

"Marcus isn't a student there anymore," she said.

"I know, Mrs. Williams. Is he all right? Is he sick? Is he okay?"

Another pause, and when she spoke again I could hear the anger in her voice. "As well as he could be, considering the stupid things he's doing with his life."

"Is he there? Can I speak to him? Is he . . . ?" I asked slowly.

"No, he's not here!" she yelled into the phone so loud I pushed it away from my ear. "He doesn't live here anymore. He lives with his grandma across town."

"Across town?" I asked. "Can I have the number?"

"Who did you say you were?" she asked, suddenly suspicious.

"I'm Nia Jones from . . . a sophomore at Endicott Academy," I said, trying to sound respectable so she wouldn't hang up.

"You said you want his grandmother's number? I don't know if I should give it to you or not. Oh, what the hell," she said, and gave me the number.

I quickly scribbled it down. What a witch, I said to myself, about to hang up the receiver, but then she spoke again, and her voice was softer.

"If you talk to him will you tell him to call me?" she said, and she hung up.

Marcus hadn't told me a lot about his mother, but I knew she'd had a lot riding on him going to Endicott, the same way Aunt Odessa had had on me. He'd said that sometimes it seemed to him that she cared more about him going to Endicott then she cared about him. I remember Marcus looking hurt when he talked about it. I also knew she didn't get along with his grandma, his father's mother.

But the sound of her voice when she'd asked him to call her — that begging sound — made me feel sorry for her. She sounded like Aunt Odessa probably would have if somebody had talked to me after I'd left Endicott — except I wouldn't have a grandmother to stay with. I'd be sitting in this apartment, looking at Aunt Odessa with her mouth poked out and Winston looking disappointed.

I dialed Marcus's grandma's number quickly. A voice said it was out of order. I dialed again. Again the recorded message. I slammed the phone down on the receiver. I dialed Marcus's mother again, but the phone was busy. I hung up and tried again; she'd probably taken it off the hook. Dead end! Everything in my life was leading to a dead end! But it couldn't stop here. Marcus must have left a clue. Somewhere, in something he'd told me or written about, there must be a clue.

I went back to the stuff I'd thrown on the bed and

started to go through it. Memories about Endicott — some good, some bad — came back. Had there been something in our last conversation that I hadn't heard? How could I not have known that he was planning to leave?

"My life is a mess," I said to the wall. "My life is a mess!" I screamed at Dandelion, who just looked at me with that blank expression on his face that he always has.

"Yeah, sister, you got that right!" I imagined him saying in the squeaky voice that I'll bet he has tucked away somewhere in his stuffings.

"My life is a mess!" I screamed at the top of my lungs to the ceiling and Mr. Lin Wan downstairs in the Chinese restaurant. As I swept the contents of my bag onto the floor in a wave of self-disgust, I spotted it.

Tucked into the reading list for Mr. Snowden's class, folded into quarters, was the first newspaper article I'd ever read about Marcus. I unfolded it slowly, and all the memories I had of him came over me. I remembered sitting on my bed that first day at Endicott, when everything was so strange and scary. Mine was the only black face I'd seen since I'd been there. I'd been afraid to open my mouth, for fear of saying something wrong, or sounding stupid, or people thinking I didn't really belong there, so I'd gone back to my room as quick as I could and closed the door. I'd opened the newspaper and there had been Marcus Garvey William's face, as brown as mine. The more I'd read that interview the better I'd felt. Yeah, I was okay; he'd come from the same place as me and *he* was making it. Marcus Garvey Williams was a star, so maybe Nia Jones could be one, too.

The interviewer who'd written the article was this kid named Anderson, who nobody could stand because they said that the only reason he was on the newspaper staff was because his daddy printed the paper for free.

> *Anderson:* Who is the greatest influence in your life?
>
> *Marcus:* My grandmother and my father.
>
> *Anderson:* What is your favorite game?
>
> *Marcus:* Chess.
>
> *Anderson:* Where did you learn to play?
>
> *Marcus:* I used to watch the old guys play in Washington Square Park in Greenwich Village. I'd get sick of being uptown and go down there to hang out. It's one of my favorite places in New York. Especially in the fall. Most people like it in the spring or summer, but I like it in the fall. Playing chess there with those old guys always cools me out, no matter what else is going down in my life.
>
> *Anderson:* So you learned how to play chess from the bums in Washington Square Park?
>
> *Marcus:* No, my father taught me how to play chess. What I learned in Washington Square Park was that there's no such thing as a bum when you face somebody

> at a chess table. Your brains count more than what you wear or where you went to school. A bum can be a rich prep with no brains, as quick as he can be a guy who learned to play chess in prison.

I could almost hear him putting Anderson in his place in that subtle, take-no-prisoners style he had. I knew Anderson calling somebody a "bum" had rubbed Marcus the wrong way, just like it had me.

"I used to go down there every Saturday to make my allowance," Marcus had told me. "I could use my smarts and make some fast cash at the same time."

Sometimes when an idea or an answer hits you it's like on those old-timey cartoons when a light bulb goes on over somebody's head. Light bulb time — that was the way I felt. Suddenly I knew where I might find Marcus.

CHAPTER ELEVEN

My aunt hardly looked at me when I "reported" to her in the kitchen. "I want you to go to the cleaners and pick up my gray suit," she said as she handed me a ticket. "And then I want you to go to the store and pick up the things I have on this list." She put the list on top of the cleaning check. "There's some towels and sheets that have to be laundered, so you can stop in there after you get back from the store, and then I want you to put on dinner. Make sure the doors are locked before you go to sleep. This should cover everything," she said as she handed me some money. I could tell by her voice that there was *no* way I could ask her permission to go into New York to find Marcus. If I'd even opened my mouth like I was going to ask something like that, she probably would have piled six more things on my "to do" list.

"Anything else you need done?" I asked, trying

not to sound fresh. She looked at me, narrowing her eyes as she finished her coffee.

"Just make sure the things I've told you to do are done correctly," she said. I sat down across from her, poured some Lucky Charms into my bowl, and opened the newspaper to the funnies. I didn't look up until I heard the door close when she left. Then I tried to figure out how I was going to do all the things she'd told me to do and still make it into New York City in time to look for Marcus. I had to go today. She wouldn't be working a double shift again for another week. Tomorrow was Saturday, and she'd be off. I got up and dressed quickly.

Of course, everything that could possibly go wrong, went wrong. The man at the cleaners couldn't find Aunt Odessa's suit, so I spent an extra half an hour waiting for him to go through every piece of clothing in the store until he found it. The laundromat we usually go to was closed, so I had to walk to one three blocks away. Everyone in a six-block radius of the place had decided to do their laundry, so I had to wait forever for a dryer — that took an extra hour. By the time I got to the grocery store, it was mid-afternoon. The checkers were so busy talking to each other about what they'd done the night before, they had to scan things two and three times before they'd take, so it took me forever to get out of there. Finally, at five everything was finished — except dinner. I figured I'd make that when I got back. By five-thirty I was making my way to Penn Station to catch the train into the city.

The day was going fast, too fast, and the sky was

getting dark. It was twilight by the time I walked out of the subway onto 14th Street, and as I headed toward Washington Square Park, I wondered if it was such a good idea after all.

During the day, I love Greenwich Village. Debra, Malika, and I had come here a couple of times together before I'd gone to Endicott, and we'd had good times. Washington Square Park is in the heart of Greenwich Village. Kids run around playing games during the day, there's always some chess players — guys like the ones Marcus used to play, and students from New York University, which is nearby, are usually sitting in the park reading or just fooling around. It's cool during the day, pleasant, and when we'd come we'd just walk around — checking out stores, watching people recite poetry and play music — but nighttime was a different story.

When I got into the park, a lot of the people who were milling around didn't look like they were there to have a good time. There was a tattered, desperate look about some of the men, and some of the kids looked mean.

"Hey, baby, can I come along?" said one scary-looking guy who was sitting on a bench. He was smoking a cigarette. I can just barely tolerate cigarettes when Aunt Odessa smokes them, so when this fool started walking next to me blowing smoke in my face, it was all I could do to keep from saying something that would have probably gotten me into trouble. I caught my breath and walked faster. It wasn't all that late, but the sun had gone down and although the streetlights were on, they didn't seem to be giving off too much light. "Hey, baby, didn't you hear me talking to you?" the cigarette-smoking fool asked. I was starting to get scared.

I walked faster. If I don't see Marcus in five minutes I'm getting my behind out of here, I thought to myself, and I started to wonder *why* he would be here in the first place. I looked around the park. There were no chess players out here tonight. Nothing but a lot of kids with nowhere to go and some scrawny, scary-looking men. If I found Marcus in the park at this time of night it meant he was probably up to no good, anyway.

I walked quickly out of the park and was just about ready to go home, when I spotted him. At least I thought it was him.

He was walking fast out of a children's clothing store, carrying a large paper bag. He looked older, and he was wearing an ancient army surplus coat that was too big for him. His hair hadn't been cut in a while and he had a mustache. For a minute, I wasn't sure that it was him, but then he crossed the street and I was sure.

"Marcus!?" I screamed out, more a question than a statement. "Marcus! Marcus!"

He looked startled and glanced in my direction. Then he started walking quicker.

"Marcus!" I screamed again. I was sure now that it was him. Some kids who looked like they were high on something pointed at me and started laughing. I didn't care; I ran after him, determined not to lose him.

He looked so different. *Could* he be doing drugs

or selling them like they'd said at Endicott? Had I been wrong and everybody else right?

"Marcus!" I yelled in a last desperate scream. I ran to keep up with him, but he was faster. He headed for a subway station, put his token in the turnstile, and ran down the stairs toward the uptown platform. Of course, I didn't have a subway token. I got in line behind this old man who couldn't find his money.

"Hurry up, hurry up, hurry up," I whispered. I didn't know I had said it so loud.

"Keep your shirt on, sister," the old man said, and gave me a dirty look.

"Sorry," I said quickly, and glanced around looking for Marcus, but he'd disappeared onto the platform. I bought a token, slipped it into the turnstile, and ran onto the platform, just as a train was pulling up. As Marcus ducked into a car, I ducked into the one behind him.

I know you're not supposed to go between trains; it's a dangerous and a stupid thing to do, but I was desperate not to lose Marcus, so I pulled back the door of my car and went into the next train. The train started vibrating and shaking just as I was between the cars. Fear, real fear, shot through me as the car rounded a corner. Somewhere in the back of my mind flashed this tale I'd heard about a kid who had been hurt switching cars. There's always the chance you're going to miss your step, miss the platform, and slip between the cars.

I pulled open the sliding door and got into Marcus's car, just as Marcus was opening his door and going into the next car. Why was he running from me? I couldn't understand it. But I knew, somehow, that if I didn't talk to him today, I would never see him again in life.

"Marcus!" I called out again. The train lurched to a stop at 135th Street, and I saw Marcus dash out of the train. I squeezed out behind him, just as the doors were closing.

He went up the subway stairs fast, and I followed. I could see the top of Marcus's head as he turned the corner and then he headed into a building. Without a second thought, I headed in, too.

It was dark in the lobby of the building — dark, close, and scary — and I stopped short the minute I was inside. It suddenly occurred to me that I didn't know where I was. I had been running and following Marcus without the faintest clue as to where I was going. It had been five when I left my house; it must be close to eight-thirty or nine now. What was I doing? Aunt Odessa would be home in three hours and . . . but before I could even form the next thought, somebody snatched me around to face him.

"What the hell do you think you're doing?" Marcus stood in front of me with his arms across his chest and a scowl on his face.

"Just what do you *think* I'm doing? I'm following you," I snapped back.

"Nia . . ." He looked at me and shook his head and then suddenly he gave me that old Marcus Garvey Williams smile. "Nia," he said again. "What do you want?"

"I want to talk to you," I said. "I want to know

what happened to you. I want to know why you left me at Endicott all by myself."

Marcus didn't say anything for a minute, and then he just grabbed and held me. I think it surprised him as much as it surprised me, because he let me go real quick.

"You followed me all the way from downtown just to find that out?" he asked.

"I followed you all the way from Endicott," I said. Although that wasn't the whole truth, it was an important part of it.

He sighed long and heavy for a moment.

"It's none of your business," he said. "And what are you doing home anyway? You're not supposed to be home until Thanksgiving."

I punched him on the arm as hard as I could. It didn't make any sense except I was mad, madder than I could remember being at anyone for a long time. And then I punched him again.

"Hey, hold on," he said. He looked at me in surprise for a moment, then he started to laugh . . . the kind of laugh he used to laugh when something was serious and he wanted to make it funny. "Okay, okay. Come on." He led me into an elevator, pushed a button, and we got off at the fifth floor. Marcus already had his key in his hand as he opened the door and led me into a small apartment. He turned to face me.

"So, Nia," he said. "You want to find out what's going on in my life? Maybe it's time you knew."

CHAPTER TWELVE

The apartment Marcus led me into was dim. A TV was on in one of the rooms, and I could hear the radiators hissing in the background. It was hot in the room, or maybe I was just nervous. Marcus motioned for me to sit down on the couch. There were neat little doilies and framed photographs of Marcus and several other kids in a straight row on a coffee table. There was also a dish filled with red-and-white candies. Peppermint, my favorite kind. My mouth watered and I started to reach for one, but then I thought better of it. It struck me that this must be his grandmother's place.

"Marcus, is that you?" a woman called from down the hall. Her voice was high.

"Yeah, Grandma."

"Who do you have with you?"

"Friend from school."

Marcus's grandmother came into the room, and I

stood to greet her. "Grandma," he said. "This is Nia Jones."

"I'm so glad to meet one of Marcus's friends," she said, and gave me a smile. Mrs. Williams was small and looked like a tiny Marcus in a weird kind of way. She had his nose, which was slightly turned up, and his eyes. Her hair circled her head in a short, soft halo that was completely gray. From the way Marcus used to talk about her, I had imagined her to be a big, strong, strapping kind of woman — kind of like Harriet Tubman in a business suit.

"How nice of you to visit Marcus," she said, but as she spoke, she looked at me closely, not mean, just curious. "But what are you doing home from school?" she asked bluntly, her eyes never leaving my face. Marcus's grandmother didn't miss a trick. I guess it struck her as strange that I was sitting in the middle of her couch, eyeing those peppermints, on a Thursday night in the middle of the school year.

"Yeah," Marcus asked, looking at me now for the answer to the questions I hadn't answered before.

I looked at them both, his grandmother waiting expectantly for my answer, and Marcus sitting with his arms crossed.

"I got kicked out for two weeks," I said simply. I was sick of lying.

There was a flicker of something in Mrs. Williams's eye. I couldn't read it, maybe sadness, maybe disappointment, I wasn't sure.

"You came to see Marcus, I guess," she said softly. "I'm going to let you-all talk." She nodded at Marcus and left the room.

Marcus waited until his grandma was out of hearing distance, and then he started in on me.

"Got kicked out for two weeks! What's wrong with you? How did you manage to get kicked out?"

I stared at him in amazement.

"Did they kick you out for real? You're going back, aren't you?"

He was beginning to sound like my aunt; I couldn't believe what I was hearing.

"What did you do? Nia, how could you risk blowing your scholarship like that?"

I couldn't take any more. "Marcus Garvey Williams, have you lost your mind?" I screamed at him as loud as I could. I'd almost forgotten I was in his grandmother's house. I stood up, shaking my finger in his face like a mad parent yelling at a bad kid. "Here you are sitting here talking about *me* getting kicked out after what *you* did. You want to know why I got kicked out of Endicott? You really want to know? Huh, huh, huh . . ."

"Nia, calm down. Calm down!"

I sat back down, glaring at him.

"Yeah, I want to know," he said after a minute. "Tell me what happened."

"You!" I yelled. "*You're* the reason I got kicked out. *You're* the reason everything has gone wrong in my life. You were supposed to be my friend. You were supposed to be in my corner, and look . . . look what's . . ." I tried to hold the tears back, but I started to cry. It was the most embarrassing thing that I could have done. Here I was, trying to tell Marcus off and suddenly the tears started coming. And I'm not talking about the kind of crying they do in movies. No, I'm talking about the real thing.

"Oh, God, Nia!" Marcus said, and he came over to where I was sitting and put his arms around me. "Nia, please don't cry." But it was too late.

"Marcus, how could you have left like that?" I cried. "Why did you leave? Where did you go? Why didn't you tell me you were going?" I looked at him, but he was all blurry.

"When you left I felt like I was all alone," I said. "Marcus, I don't have that many people in my corner. I just don't. There's my aunt, my girls, and there was you, and when . . ."

"Nia," he said. "I — "

"Why, Marcus, why?"

But before he could answer a cry came from another part of the apartment. I realized it was a baby crying, and I looked at Marcus, puzzled. He got up and went to the rear of the apartment, and he didn't come back for a few minutes. When he did he was holding a baby.

"Nia," he said. "Meet Maurice. I named him after my father. This is my son."

My mouth dropped open, and for a minute I couldn't close it. No words came out. I sat there for about thirty seconds without saying anything. "What?" I finally managed to ask.

Marcus cocked his head and smiled that Marcus smile — the one he'd smiled that first night when I'd met him, and that night when he'd said good-bye in McCarter's Woods — the one that could make you forgive him and like him no matter what you'd felt before.

"My son, Nia." He handed the baby to me, and, despite my feelings about babies, I took him and held him. He had that sweet, soft smell — baby powder mixed with burped-up milk — that babies always seem to have, and as I looked into his eyes I felt myself smiling, too.

"Marcus?" I said, but I didn't know what else to say. For the first time in my life, I understood what the word *speechless* meant.

Marcus went to the kitchen and came back with a bottle filled with formula. He took the baby from me and stuck the bottle into his mouth with one smooth motion — like an expert. Then he settled back against the couch like he'd been holding Maurice all his life. The only noise in the room was the sound of Marcus's son making quick work of that bottle. Finally Marcus started talking, slow and carefully, like he was telling me a story or remembering a dream.

"You remember, Nia, how I didn't call you last summer?" he asked.

"Do I remember my name?"

Marcus glanced at me sideways, hearing the disappointment that was still in my voice, and sighed.

"Last summer was a real bust for me," he said. "Remember I used to talk about this girl, Betty, who lived across the hall from my mom?"

I thought back and couldn't really recall him mentioning anybody named Betty. "She's the mother?" I asked.

"Well," Marcus said, not looking at me. "I had this thing going with Betty. It was like real quick, you know. Last January, you know when I was home during semester break, me and Betty used to fool around a lot. Her mom wasn't home one Friday, you know, and we were there by ourselves. I don't think it meant that much to either of us."

"It means something now, I guess," I said. I wasn't trying to be mean, but it struck me that Marcus should have known better. "You didn't use anything with all this AIDS mess and everything?" I asked.

"Nia," Marcus said with a typically Marcus look. "If I had, would we be sitting here now having this conversation?"

No, that was for sure. I had to give him that.

"Well," he continued. "Anyway, Betty got pregnant. She told me it was mine, but I really didn't believe her, and my mom said *not* to believe her, so I tried not to. But it was still scary, you know what I mean?"

I didn't know what he meant, but I nodded my head like I did.

Marcus held the baby up to burp him and laid him on his shoulder. "So anyway," he continued, "that was pretty much the way it went all summer. Betty telling me it was my baby. My mom telling me to forget about it. Me deciding that I just didn't want to deal with it at all. I just tried to forget the whole thing. But I couldn't. It was like the worst time of my life. I stayed in my room reading, thinking, wasting time all summer. Dev called a couple of times and I didn't call him back. And you . . ."

"It's okay," I said to Marcus. "It's okay."

"Maurice was born on September 1. The week before school started. Betty's mother insisted that I take a blood test to prove that the baby was mine. My mom told me *not* to take it, but I took it anyway; I had to know." Marcus held his son up and kissed him on the forehead. "He's mine," he said softly.

We sat there quietly for a minute, neither of us saying anything. The baby was making those funny sounds that babies make.

"Those first two days of school were really strange," Marcus went on. "I was going through the motions — talking to people, joking around, making plans for the future, but everything in my life had changed. I thought I could make it. The baby was here; I was there. You know how Endicott is like another world?"

"Yeah," I said with a knowing nod. "How well I know."

"Well, I thought I could just forget about him, you know, go on with my life like a lot of guys do when a girl has a baby they don't want. But then I got this call from my grandmother. It was a couple of days before I left. Grandma told me that Betty had run away from home and left the baby with her mother. Her mother was thinking about giving the baby away, you know, putting him in social services. Nobody wanted him around. Nobody."

Marcus hugged his son, like the very thought of nobody wanting him, of giving him away, scared him. "I talked to my mom. She'd told me that the whole thing wasn't my fault. That he was Betty's responsibility. That I had my life now. I had a future. I was going places and there was no need for me to let things hold me back. When I got to be a man I could send them some money, but school was most important."

"Your mom said all that? That's cold," I said. I didn't mean to dis Marcus's mom like that, but it struck me as really being mean for her to put down her grandson.

"Yeah, it does sound that way now," Marcus said with a little chuckle. "But I think she was as messed up about this whole thing as I was. At first I tried to act like she did; cold, kind of. And then I started dreaming about my father. Remember when we were sitting in McCarter's Woods that time and I told you about when he left?"

"Yeah."

"I had been dreaming about him the whole two weeks before that. When I'd wake up sometimes I'd be crying. I'd started to think about how much he'd meant to me. What a difference he'd made in my life. And I started to think about Maurice. He wasn't named Maurice then because nobody even had named him, and I knew that I owed him. Because Maurice is part of my daddy, the same way he's part of me, and I couldn't just throw him away.

"When you saw me in the cafeteria that day that I asked you for the money, I had decided to catch the early morning train back to New York City. I used your fifty dollars for that."

"Wow," I said quietly. "What are you doing now?" I asked him.

"I'm taking care of my son," he said simply. "When I left Endicott, my mom tried to convince me to go back. When I wouldn't, she told me I could stay with her, but I couldn't bring my son to live with us. I got Maurice and I came here to live with Grandma. Maybe my mom will come around someday. But I had to do what I had to do."

As if on cue, the baby started to cry, and Marcus patted him. I still couldn't get used to seeing him with a baby.

"Marcus," his grandmother said as she came back into the room. "Go around to the store on the corner and see if they have any formula." Marcus stood up and handed Maurice to her. "Ready to go?" he asked me, and I took it by his tone that *he* was ready for me to go. "I'll walk you to the subway stop."

"Okay," I said as I put on my coat. "Nice to have met you," I said to Marcus's grandmother. I gave Maurice a peck on the cheek. I always forget how soft and warm babies are, and how fragile.

"Ready?" Marcus said as he gestured toward the door.

As he closed the door behind us and headed toward the street, I walked fast to keep up with him.

CHAPTER THIRTEEN

"Slow down," I said impatiently. After the mad dash uptown, I was sick of running after him. "I've found you now. I know all your business. There's no sense in trying to get away from me." Marcus chuckled, but he slowed down.

"Did you really think that I was just going to forget about you and never wonder about why you left or what became of you?" I asked.

"I guess I was hoping that you would. That's why I was trying to get away from you in the Village. I felt like I'd let you down, let everybody down . . . except Maurice. I felt kind of bad for a while."

"How are you feeling now?"

"Well, most of the time I feel good. I'm going to make it. Everything is going to be okay." We walked a little further without saying anything.

"Are you dropping out of high school?" I finally

asked. All Maurice needed was a high school dropout for a father, but I didn't say that.

"Do I look like a high school dropout?" He gave me that old Marcus look.

"I'm a security guard for a kids' clothing store," he said. "The money's not great but it's more than I could make playing chess in the park, and I can get clothes at a good discount for my son."

It still sounded strange to hear Marcus talking about "my son."

"Are you ever going to go back to Endicott?" I asked. "They'll probably let you back in, after all . . ." Marcus stopped short and turned to confront me. For a minute I thought he was going to yell at me, but he didn't.

"I can't take Maurice to Endicott," he said quietly. "Endicott is in my past." We started walking again. "Listen, Nia, Endicott is not the only road for me. I'm more determined to make it now than I ever was at Endicott." Marcus picked up a can and tossed it into the street. It made a tinny sound as it bounced against the curb and rolled into the gutter.

"How?" I asked. I didn't mean to sound doubtful, but that was how I was feeling. Exactly *how* was he going to take care of his son and go to school?

"Remember that law firm, the one with those black lawyers on West 121st Street where I interned last summer?"

"Yeah."

"Well, they liked me then, and they remembered me. I'm working as an office boy, starting next week.

It took me a while to find a job, you know, without my high school diploma and stuff — I was playing a lot of chess in Washington Square Park — but I remembered them, and they remembered me, and Mr. Errol, the head of the firm, is going to be helping me out. I can put in some time Saturdays at the clothes store, too."

"But what about school?"

"I talked about what went down with Mr. Errol. He's on the board of trustees at Endicott, and he says that since I was an advanced placement student last year and finished up most of the courses there, he's going to call Hagen, explain what's happened, and see if I get the couple of credits I need from another school. I can still get my diploma from Endicott. Grandma has some money saved from my father's insurance policy, and we're making it. Things are tight, but we're making it, and she takes good care of Maurice." We walked a little further and he nodded to a couple of guys sitting on the stoop.

"You know I can take any test — high school equivalency or anything else they throw my way, and pass it with my eyes closed," he said.

I nodded in agreement. That I was sure of.

"I got good SAT scores when I took them last year. I'm getting mail from a lot of colleges who are interested in giving me money to go there." He hesitated for a moment. "Me and Maurice are going to be okay."

I looked at him for a moment and I knew that he would be. We went into a small store and got some formula for Maurice. Marcus checked the expiration date on the formula before he bought it. Then he got two sodas. We sat down on the stairs of a building near the store to drink them.

"I told you what happened to me. Now tell me your story," he said between sips.

I took a deep breath and told him everything — from the fight, to the trip to Hagen's office, to my hard times with Aunt Odessa and my girls Debra and Malika.

"So you're not going back?" he asked at the end of my tale.

"No," I said. "Just like *you* decided, *I* decided. I don't fit in anymore." I gulped down my soda so fast I almost choked.

"Nia, not going back isn't the answer."

"It was the answer for you, why isn't it for me?"

"Everyone's answer is different. My answer isn't your answer. I have a kid now. I have a responsibility. Your responsibility is still just you."

We tossed the soda cans into a nearby trash can and started walking again.

"So you think I should go back?"

"It's your decision. But you've got a full scholarship to the best prep school in the country." We both started laughing at that. That "best prep school in the country" mess always made us laugh. It was like old times for a minute.

"Go on, Aunt Odessa," I said.

Marcus was suddenly serious again. "We both know Endicott is full of crap, but it's one of the best. You've got to give it its due."

"Marcus, I feel like I'm losing myself there. As long

as I'm there, I'm less Nia Jones. I'm afraid I'll come out somebody else. When you were there I could always be sure of who I was — you were the same kind of kid as me. If you could make it, I could."

"You don't have to give up who you are to go to Endicott," Marcus said. "I didn't, I never will. I am Marcus Garvey Williams." He thumped himself on the chest half in jest. "I am an African-American male. Son of Maurice Williams. Father of Maurice Marcus Williams . . . friend of Nia Jones. I knew why I was there, just like you have to know why you are there."

"I'm not sure," I said. I didn't mean to whine, but that was the truth.

"Think about your name, Nia. *Purpose*. Think about all the things there are to be done." He looked around the block and waved his arms in the direction of one of the burned-out buildings. A little kid was jumping rope by herself in front of it. It was nearly eleven, but she was there all by herself and the rope was thumping on the sidewalk, the only sound besides me and Marcus talking. I wondered where her parents were, why she would be jumping rope by herself at this time of night.

"So many of the guys I went to grammar school with are dead now," Marcus said. "I *have* to make it. You do, too."

"Marcus, everything about that place is strange," I said, forgetting about the kid jumping rope. "I don't even have any friends there, I — "

"Nia, that's garbage. Sometimes you're the one who cuts people out. Sometimes you're a snob, too.

Remember that first square dance last year? How you came in scared, not talking to anybody, and then how you started having a good time, remember — "

"Marcus, you were there then."

"Yeah, you opened up to me because we were both on scholarship and all that. We had a lot in common. But I had things in common with Dev, too. He wasn't hardly on nobody's scholarship. You'll find kids you have stuff in common with, too."

"Yeah, Marcus, sure," I said. We walked into the subway station, and Marcus put in two tokens so we could wait for the train together. As we leaned against the subway wall waiting for the train to come, I felt like crying. "Marcus," I said instead, "I love you." Saying those words surprised me as much as they surprised Marcus, but they seemed like the right thing to say.

"I love you too, Nia," he said quickly, like he was embarrassed. Then he turned his eyes and focused on the track waiting for the train. When we could hear it coming, he glanced at me for a second and he gave me a long hug. I hugged him back as hard as I could. When I got into the train I stood at the door. "Nia," Marcus called out as the door was closing. "Friends for life?"

"For life," I yelled back, and I watched him head up the stairs and back into the street.

CHAPTER FOURTEEN

I felt good on the way home, like you do when you've found something that you lost a long time ago. I thought I had some answers. When I got home, I heated up a can of baked beans and broiled some hot dogs for Aunt Odessa to eat. It wasn't much of a dinner, and I felt bad about that, but I was just glad to be home before she was. I left it in the oven. Just as my head was hitting the pillow, my aunt's key turned in the lock. I heard her come into the kitchen and put some things down on the table. Her chair scraped against the floor as she sat down, and I heard her sigh.

She sounded tired. I had never realized how tired she got after a double shift. (I'm usually asleep.) I got up and came into the kitchen. Aunt Odessa was sitting at the table with her head in her hands. For a minute I thought she was crying, and then I realized she was asleep. I stood watching her for a moment, and then I quietly sat down across from her. I thought about all those times when she'd come home and I'd been in bed — all those times when she'd probably fallen asleep at the kitchen table and I hadn't known it. Those times when I'd been little and she'd worked double shifts and cooked, ironed, cleaned, worried about me, and I'd never even said thank you.

I leaned over and kissed her on the forehead.

"Ooomph," she said with a start, and her eyes popped open. "Go on back to sleep. I'm going to heat up my dinner and go to bed," she said as she put her chin back in her hands and closed her eyes again.

I put the hot dogs and beans on a plate and made a little salad of lettuce and tomato with a dab of salad dressing on it. I put on some water for tea, and then I sat back down across from her. She looked up and gave me a half-smile. I wondered if she was still mad at me. I thought that she probably was, but I didn't care anymore. I watched her eat, lifting each forkful as if it were heavy. She finished half her plate and then sipped her tea. "I'm getting too old for this double-shift mess," she said. "Just too darn old."

She really did look older. There were gray hairs I'd never noticed before. I wondered how long it would be before she'd have as much gray hair as Marcus's grandmother.

"Aunt Odessa," I said. I had to say it twice because she had settled her head back into her hands again and was dozing. "Aunt Odessa?"

"Yeah."

"I . . ." I wasn't really sure what to say. I wanted to ask her about Winston, if they were living together while I wasn't here, and I wanted to tell her about Marcus and Maurice and Debra and Malika. But the words didn't come.

"Yeah?" she asked again, her eyes probing mine for an answer.

"I just wanted to tell you not to bother asking Winston to rent another car to take me back to Endicott on Sunday. I can take the train, it will drop me off at the station, and I can use that fifty dollars he gave me before to take a cab from the station to the school."

I don't know when I'd made the decision to go back to Endicott. I just knew that it had been made, and going back was as right for me at this point in my life as *not* going back was for Marcus. Sitting there, looking at Aunt Odessa eating her dinner, I realized that I owed her. I owed her big. She wanted Endicott for me, and even if I wasn't sure that I wanted it for myself, I had to give it another shot . . . for her.

"Are you sure?" she asked, and I knew she was asking not only if I were sure about going back on the train but about Endicott, only she didn't want to say that. "We don't mind taking you back."

"Yeah, I'm sure," I said.

"I can sure use Sunday to catch up on some sleep," she said. She looked at me for a moment and then smiled a slow smile — the kind she used to smile when I'd gotten an A on a term paper or won a prize. A proud smile.

When my aunt was finished eating, I scraped the food from her plate into the trash. She gave me a good-night kiss and went into her bedroom and closed the door. And as I filled the sink with detergent to wash the dishes and the scent of lemon bubbles tickled my nose, I felt good. I was dead tired, but I felt good, really good.

I spent the next day, Saturday, reviewing some chemistry notes that I'd put off looking at, thinking I wasn't going back. Saturday night I washed, ironed, and packed the clothes that I always wore at Endicott and that I thought I'd never use again. And at eleven o'clock on Sunday, Aunt Odessa took me to the train station.

She bought me a candy bar and a can of soda at the newspaper stand when we got there. I really didn't want them, but I took them anyway so I wouldn't hurt her feelings. Then she walked me up to the platform and we waited for the train to come.

"I'm proud of you, Nia," she said, and she gave me a hug and kiss. I hugged her back as tightly as I could and took a bite of the candy bar so I wouldn't cry. When the train came I got on quick, but my aunt stood on the platform waiting for me to find a seat. When I found one, she walked over to where I was sitting.

"Good-bye," she mouthed through the glass. It was a different kind of "good-bye" than other times. I guess there are lots of different ways to say good-bye. I watched her disappear as the train pulled out of the station, and I kept watching even though she was gone. Then I settled back into my seat, heading back to Endicott Academy.

Just as the train was pulling out I felt panic, pure and cold and simple. How could I face everybody again — everybody knowing I'd been suspended. Maybe it was better just to stay here — living the old life, knowing the old people. But I thought about Debra and Malika, and about Winston and my aunt, and thought again how different things were.

But, of course, life wasn't about to let me live it in peace — it threw me another curve. Just as the train was pulling out, just when it was too late to go to another car or wait for another train, who came strolling down the aisle, looking for a seat, but Lucinda Spinotta.

We both looked frantically around the car — both of us hoping she could find somewhere else to sit. No luck. As she walked back to where I was, I gazed out the window, determined not to say anything.

She spoke first. "Can I sit here, Nia?" she asked. It was the first time I had ever heard her say my name.

"Yeah, I guess so," I said, with an attitude. "I only paid for one seat, the one I'm sitting in." She sat down.

We both looked straight ahead, not saying anything for the first fifteen minutes, and I silently cursed my luck. But then I decided that this was as good a time as any to clear Marcus's name — since she was the person who had had the most to say about him in the first place. I cleared my throat.

"Lucinda Spinotta," I said more loudly than I meant to. "I think you should know that I saw Marcus Garvey Williams this week, and he wants everyone — including you — at Endicott to know that he is doing *just fine*. He's finishing high school on time, colleges are already chasing him, and he is going to be a lawyer like he always said he would. There were reasons, personal reasons, why he had to leave. He had family . . . responsibilities." I said it formally, like a speech, with a Hagen flourish and nod of my head. "And furthermore," I said, my voice lowering a notch, looking her straight in the eye. "Marcus *never used drugs*."

"I'm sorry, Nia," Lucinda said quietly. "Tell Marcus I'm sorry I said those things about him."

I noticed the scratch on the side of her face and suddenly I felt bad about putting it there. I realized that I'd hurt her as much as she'd hurt me. I noticed she was looking at the scratch over my left eye. I guess we both carried scars. I noticed the triple-pierced holes in her ears that I'd spotted for the first time on the bus. Funny how seeing them again reminded me how little I knew her.

"I feel out of place sometimes at Endicott," she said after a few minutes. "I feel like . . . well, you know, everybody's rich and when I tell them about my parents they're always saying things like we're in the mob, joking, you know, but it still cuts deep, real deep. And I feel real bad about myself sometimes." She swallowed and then continued. "Sometimes I talk about people, about you and Marcus, sometimes it makes me feel more like I belong, like I'm not just a . . ."

"Poor, dumb kid from the inner city on scholarship?" I asked.

"Yeah," she said, with an ironic chuckle. "Like a poor, dumb kid from the inner city on scholarship." We sat there for a few moments, not saying anything, and when Lucinda spoke again it was as if she were telling me a secret.

"Things were different at home this time," she said. "I didn't really fit in there, either. My best friend is going to cosmetology school. Another one of my friends is working at the mall, and she thinks that's a big thing. I think I might be more at home at Endicott at this point than I am there."

"I know what you mean," I said quietly.

"And you know, the guys . . ." She rolled her eyes in disgust. "The guys you meet . . . like that bozo on the bus."

"The bus!" I said and covered my face with my hands in embarrassment relived. The memory made us both groan.

" 'Were you in Mrs. Perry's class?' " Lucinda said suddenly, doing a dead-to-right imitation of me.

I looked at her in surprise and noticed the twinkle in her eye. Not to be outdone, I smacked my lips in an imitation of a kiss. And then we both started to giggle, softly at first, shyly.

" 'Fingerpainting was always my favorite,' " Lucinda said teasingly.

" 'Tony . . .' " I said in a fake, seductive drawl. "At least I didn't kiss *him*!"

Lucinda started laughing and put her finger in her mouth pretending to gag, and for a moment, just for a moment, she reminded me of Debra. And then we both began to laugh — that kind of rip-roaring howl that makes your stomach ache and the people around you lower their newspapers and look at you in disgust. We laughed until the conductor sneered at us, and an old lady with blue hair in a tacky fur coat turned around and said "Hush." And then we stopped just long enough to start laughing again.

"I'll never forget that as long as I live," Lucinda said. "I wasn't going to come back, you know. I was going to stay at home, maybe go to school, maybe hang out with my friends, but then I realized . . . that I couldn't do that."

We were quiet after that, both of us lost in our own thoughts, but when the train pulled into the station, we pooled our money and decided we'd share a cab back to Endicott. It was cheaper that way.

I don't know if Lucinda and I will be friends. I don't know if she'll change now that we're back at Endicott, or if I will, or even if either of us will make it through the year — though considering what we've both been through, we've got a pretty good chance. But I do know that it felt good to laugh again, and that anyone who I can laugh with that hard can't be all bad — maybe more like me than I thought.

I think a lot about Marcus these days. We write to each other about once a month and, from what he tells me, he and Maurice are doing fine . . . just like he said they would. I think a lot about Malika and Debra, too. I wonder if Malika will get the money she needs for college and if Debra will ever see through that fool she's going out with. I wrote them both when I got back, but I haven't heard from either one yet.

Maybe someday one or both of them will call me and we can take up where we left off. But then again, maybe not. I know one thing for sure, though. They'll always be as much a part of me as my parents, Aunt Odessa, and Marcus. That won't change. People you love always leave some part of themselves with you, even when they're gone.